This Thug Love Got Me Trippin:
A Belize Christmas

By

Princess Diamond

Twitter & Instagram: @authorprincess
Facebook: @authorprincessdiamond
Pinterest: princess diamond
Snap Chat: prettysexystyle

This Thug Love Got Me Trippin: A Belize Christmas Copyright © 2018 Princess Diamond

Acknowledgements

I give all praises to God who anointed me with this wonderful gift of writing. Through Christ I can do all things.

To my father in heaven, you passed away too soon. You have never seen any of my work, but I write in your memory. Love always.

To my mother in heaven, I still can't believe you're gone so soon. I miss you every day. I wish you were here with me. My biggest supporter. Love Always.

To my family and friends, I couldn't have done this without your endless days of listening to me talk about my stories, offering ideas, and giving me advice. You all are my rock. Thanks for everything.

To all the authors that have helped me. From giving me advice to supporting my work to the positive interactions. Much love.

To my readers, without your support, there is no me. I appreciate you all.

A special thanks to my sisters. Your input is priceless.

XOXOX
Princess Diamond

♛ Princess Diamond's Books ♛

Chapter 1

Ace Hood

"You're not about to lie in bed all day," my mother said, barging into my bedroom.

"Get out," I exclaimed with the pillow over my head. My mother snatched the pillow and I snatched it right back. "Go away."

"Listen, boy, you're not the first person to fall down on your luck."

"I don't want the speech, Ma. I just want to lay here and sleep my life away."

"You must be crazy if you think your father and I raised you like that. So what, you lost a few things."

"A few things?" I repeated. "Ma, I lost my whole life and you're acting like it's no big deal."

Princess Diamond

"I cooked you breakfast. The least you can do is shower and come down and eat. After that, you can start looking for a job because you're not going to stay in my place rent free. No sir. Your father and I didn't raise you like that. You have to stand on your own two feet."

"Ugggggh!" I groaned. "How many times are you going to tell me that?"

"As many times as you need to hear it until it sinks in."

"Ma, you're not making this any better, okay? Preaching to me just makes me feel worse."

My mother flopped down on my bed and sighed. "I think it was that hussy that you were seeing that got you into all this mess. Your life was on track before you got engaged to her."

"Now, you're bringing up old stuff, ma. I'm trying my best to move on, not slit my wrists," I stated sarcastically.

"Whatever boy. Shower and get dressed so you can come down and eat. When you're done, you can straighten up this room and make this bed. You know I don't play. You know I don't like a messy house."

This Thug Love Got Me Trippin: A Belize Christmas

"Yes, ma'am."

As soon as my mother closed the door, I turned over and contemplated going back to sleep until my stomach growled. I was hungry as fuck after the wild ass night that I had. I barely made it home. In fact, I don't even remember making it home. I remember being at the club popping bottles and then waking up in my bed from my mama's loud voice.

I tried to go back to sleep and it wasn't working. My brain was awake, even though my body wasn't. A million thoughts rushed through my head. Getting out of bed, I adjusted my dick, yawned, stretched, and started cleaning up my room. Next, I made my bed and showered before I headed downstairs to the kitchen.

My mother left a note that said she was gone to work, but my breakfast was on the stove. She made my favorite: wheat pancakes, turkey sausage, and a veggie omelet. My boys clowned me about my eating, but I had to stay fit. Diabetes ran deep on both sides of my family. I didn't want that shit, so I did what I had to do. I watched what I ate and exercised religiously.

After eating, I went for a jog through the

3

neighborhood. My mother lived in Evergreen. It was pretty decent. I grew up here my whole life so the crime in Chicago didn't bother me. Most of the people around this way I knew. I was pretty popular from my street days, so I wasn't worried about the bullshit that others faced here in the city. Chicks loved me and dudes wanted to be me.

It was nearly four in the afternoon by the time I returned to my parents' house. I ran into a few of my buddies and ended up shooting the shit. I got a fresh haircut too. My mother didn't come home until almost eight. She worked 2nd shift and my father was a truck driver. He always worked doubles, so he was never at home. I let myself in and jogged upstairs. I was exhausted, so I took a nap. When I woke up, it was almost eight. My mother would be walking in around nine, so I had to disappear before she got here. I didn't want her talking me out of partying tonight. I'd been partying every night since I moved in and she was already sick of it.

Checking my phone, I noticed that I had a few texts. One from my cousin Cakes asking me how I was doing. He'd been checking on me every day since the breakup. My fiancée left me

This Thug Love Got Me Trippin: A Belize Christmas

after I lost my job. She packed all of her shit in the middle of the night and I hadn't heard or seen her ass since. She changed her number and everything. Family members had been telling me that she was a gold digging ass hoe, but I loved her. I guess I was too blind to see her for who she really was.

I didn't text him back. I didn't want to hear the pity in his voice. We were raised like brothers, so he knew when I was faking it and when I was real. Right now, I was faking it because my life was in shambles. I just wanted to go out and drink my problems away. Alcohol numbed my pain. Yeah, that sounded real stupid considering things could be much worse.

My mother said I should be counting my blessings. I heard her voice clear as day. Right now, all of my mother's church mumbo jumbo didn't seem to apply. I grew up in the church and I loved God. However, it seemed like as soon as I started to do the right thing, I was slapped in the face. Forgive me if I wasn't feeling the Christian way. My prayers went unanswered. I asked for a woman who loved me for me and being my own boss. Instead, I got a fiancée who left me for dead. I lost my job and my crib. In six months, everything that I had obtained went straight to hell and I found myself back at my parents' spot, crashing.

I answered my phone, "Aye."

"Dawg, Toki has been asking about you day and night."

"Word?" I asked with a smile on my face. Toki was a bad bitch. She could help me forget about anything that I was stressing over.

"Nicca, she done asked everyone we know about your crusty ass."

I laughed. My boy Trike was crazy as hell.

"She wanted to know if you're coming out tonight or what?

"Tell her, I'll be there."

"Good because she sounds like she's down for whatever."

"That's good because I'm down for whatever too."

"What you gone do? I would make her bring one of her fine ass friends and get my threesome on."

"Bruh, a good nicca never kisses and tells."

"Your ass ain't good," Trike joked. "If

you're good, then I'm an angel."

"You have to go to church in order to be an angel."

"Stop playing. I go to church more than your heathen ass."

I cracked up. "On the real, I'm coming out tonight. Tell Toki I'll be there."

"Bruh, I already told her. I know you better than you think. You're my boy and we've been boys since forever. I knew what you wanted me to tell her, so I already said that shit. Now, get your stanking ass in the shower. I'm sure you just got back from running."

I chuckled. "You better stop talking about me before I call your baby mama."

"You should have just shot me. That would be better than hearing her mouth."

I cracked up because I knew he was serious. "You're a fool. I thought you loved her."

"Nicca, I do, but she's crazy as hell. Sometimes, I just need a break."

I continued to laugh at his misery. "What time are we meeting up?"

"In an hour."

"Cool. That gives me time to shower and

dress."

"Aight. I'll see you there, Ace."

"No doubt."

I hung up and went to figure out what I wanted to wear. Toki was going to be there, so I had to be fly. I wasn't looking for a girlfriend or nothing, but she would make a good jump off. She was cute, had her own money, and her own crib. Since I was back living at home with my parents, I needed to fool around with a chick who had her own shit.

I got to the bar around eleven. I would have been here sooner, but I couldn't remember where I parked my car. My car note was way past due and the repo man was out on the prowl. Every time I drove home, I had to park my shit far away, in different spots each time. I was hiding my car from the repo man and half the time I couldn't find it my damn self. Sometimes, it took me ten minutes walking around for blocks before I remembered where it was.

"About time you made it," Trike said. "I ain't think your ass was gonna show."

They were already taking shots when I joined in.

This Thug Love Got Me Trippin: A Belize Christmas

I laughed. "Shit, I almost didn't. I couldn't find my ride."

"Not again," he laughed, along with the rest of my boys.

Trike pushed another shot my way. "Nicca, you need this shit. Your life is so fucked up. You've lost your job, your girl, your crib, and you're ass is about to lose your damn car."

"Don't remind me. I've been putting in job applications like crazy, but ain't shit came through yet."

"It's the holidays, bruh. You'll get something afterwards. Until then, drink up."

We were knocking those shots back when I heard a sweet voice call my name.

"Hey, Ace," Toki said, walking up, taking a seat by me. "I see you made it out tonight."

I grinned and nodded coolly. "No doubt. Good to see you."

I leaned over and gave her a hug. She giggled, hugged me back, and ordered another round of shots. Toki was a wild girl. After she asked me to take body shots from her cleavage, she invited me to the dance floor and threw her ass on me. We were pretty much fucking with our clothes on. By the time the bar closed around three am, I was ready to go back to Toki's spot and fuck her senseless.

"Are you ready for the night to end?" I asked Toki smoothly,

"No," she replied with a purr. "I was hoping you would come back to my place and keep the party going."

I smirked. "That's what I thought." As much as she rubbed all up on me, she knew I was packing. Some dudes bragged on their dicks, but I didn't have to. The chicks that I dated bragged on my manhood for me.

"Text me your address and I'll be on my way after I say bye to my boys."

Toki pressed her body against mine and tongued me down something proper. If she fucked the way she kissed, I was in for a real treat.

"Don't keep me waiting," she said. "I can't wait for you to show me what you're working with."

I smiled on the outside but, on the inside, I was gloating. I'd pulled some bad broads, but Toki was next level fine.

This Thug Love Got Me Trippin: A Belize Christmas

"I'ma slide through as soon as I holla at them."

She blew me a kiss and switched out the door. Her booty was bouncing out of control and I could tell she didn't have any panties on. My dick was already starting to swell and I couldn't wait to beat her pussy up. I ain't had no head or nothing since my fiancée left me. I wouldn't say that I was depressed like my boys claimed. It was more like I didn't trust bitches anymore. I just needed time.

"You out?" Trike asked me.

"Yep. I'm about to knock down them walls," I replied with a smirk.

"My man," one of my other boys said, giving me some dap.

"Cool," Trike said. "Make sure you strap up."

"Always."

I did a few more shots with my boys and staggered out of the bar. The night air was cold, so I gripped on my jacket while trying to find out where I parked my car. For a minute, I thought the repo man had got me because I couldn't find my car for shit.

Princess Diamond

Finally, I remembered that I re-parked my ride after seeing a closer spot. Sighing in relief, I got in and pulled off. I hopped on the Dan Ryan and realized I didn't know where I was going. I was so fucked up that I was about to drive home. Reaching in my back pocket, I pulled out my phone and then fumbled with it to unlock the screen. It might be early in the morning, but traffic was booming for a Thursday. It was as if niccas had called in so they could start the weekend early. As soon as I unlocked my phone, I dropped it.

"Fuck!" I hollered, reaching down to grab it.

I was steering the wheel and peeking at traffic while feeling around on the floor for my damn phone. My car was bobbing and weaving in and out of lanes and a few cars honked at me. I was just about to get off on the nearest exit when I saw the familiar red and blue flashing lights.

"Got Damn! I can't win for losing."

Quickly, I pulled my car over on the side of the Dan Ryan, and got my license and registration, since I knew the officer would want it.

"License and registration," the white officer

asked boldly with his hand near his gun.

I didn't want to be shot, so I slowly handed him my information. He used his flashlight to observe what I had given him. "Where are you coming from son?"

I hated when people called me son like I was their kid or sum. I bit my jaw before answering. "Hanging with some friends."

"Were you drinking?"

Fuck! "I had a drink or two," I said, lying my ass off. I had about two million drinks.

"Get out of the car."

"Is that really necessary?"

When the police officer put his hand near his gun again, I reassured him that I would cooperate.

"Fine. I'm getting out. Just don't shoot."

Slowly getting out with my hands in the air, I missed my step and fell face first on the ground. As wasted as I was, I started laughing and I couldn't stop. I don't know why I found this funny, but I did. An image of me rolling around on the ground trying to get up was all I could think of.

The officer bent down with a breathalyzer in his hand and had me blow into the mouthpiece. I could barely breathe into it because I had the chuckles and I couldn't stop. It was true what they said in the hood. I was laughing so hard to keep myself from crying. I knew I was fucked when his eyes popped open wide after reading the results.

"You're under arrest for driving while under the influence," the officer announced, cuffing me. He helped me off the ground and put me into the back of the police car.

And if that shit wasn't bad enough, the repo man pulled up as we were driving off and towed my damn car away. I was royally fucked.

Chapter 2

Cassie "Sassy" Treyton

I was that pretty girl that was raised in a wealthy family with my younger brother Eli. We had loads of money at our disposal. My brother had always been the rebel and I was the princess. Our parents didn't come from money, but they definitely scraped and saved until they had all the money they could ever want. Needless to say, we grew up with the most lavish things.

My parents grew up poor on the Southside of Chicago, so they were what people would call "new money." Sometimes, they acted like they'd had money all of their lives and, other times, the ratchet Southside came out and people would catch these hands.

Princess Diamond

My mother Clara Treyton was a psychiatrist and she evaluated everyone. She never left her job at work. She dissected everyone she spoke to, trying to get in their head, diagnose them, and figure out what their issues were. My father Liam Treyton was an award-winning cardiac surgeon. People flew from all over the world to make appointments with him. My parents decided to invest their money so that they could help take care of their families and everyone could win. Now, they are both rich business owners of a popular fast food chain and a well-known coffee shop throughout the United States.

I loved my parents with all of my heart, but being their princess was a blessing and a curse. My parents liked things a certain way and they didn't understand change too well. You see, my parents were old fashion. They believed in all the family traditions. Sex before marriage. A man should be a provider. Babies before thirty. And, of course, Christmas was a big deal. The over the top and extravagant holiday that they lived for every year. How could I tell them that I wasn't coming to their fabulous Christmas dinner because I didn't have a boyfriend? Because I felt

This Thug Love Got Me Trippin: A Belize Christmas

ashamed and unworthy as a woman because I was single, lonely, and all I had was my career.

I looked down at my phone, which rang for the hundredth time today. I sighed. I wanted to scream, but I was at work and that wouldn't be possible. Finally, I swiped the call button and answered my phone since it wouldn't stop ringing.

"Yes, mom," I said with an apparent attitude.

I held my phone tight while rushing to the break room, so I could speak in private. Taking the call at my desk would have been career suicide. My coworkers were way too nosey anyway. Besides, I just started this job so I wanted to keep them out of my business.

"It's about time you picked up," my mother voiced through the phone. "For a minute, I thought you were trying to avoid me. Why do I have to call you all the time, Sassy? Why can't you just pick up your phone like a normal daughter and call your mama without her calling you? I worry about you, girl."

"Mom, why would I avoid you?" I replied with a snarl. She was right on the money. I was avoiding her like the plague. I didn't need the stress.

"I can't be mad because you're probably boo'd up with your new boo. You do have a boyfriend, right?"

I rolled my eyes to the ceiling. My mother was always in my love life. She felt as if I should have been married at eighteen like she was.

"Mom, I have no idea what you're talking about right now. You're just being nosey."

"Maybe I am, but you're my baby. I can dig as deep as I want to. You know that I want you to be happy, honey. By now, you should be married with a family of your own."

"Mom don't start."

"I don't want you to be old and lonely. I don't want you to wait until you're too old to get pregnant. Nobody is going to want you."

"I don't want to hear this mess, mama."

"I'm just saying, all of your friends are married or engaged. When do I get to see you walk down the aisle? I'm getting old for heaven's sake."

"You're only forty-six, mom. You're still young. In fact, you're young enough to still have a baby." I really didn't want another sibling. I just wanted her to get off my back about marriage and babies.

"Damn that. I wouldn't dare mess up my figure after all this work that I've gotten done to look this incredible. It's your time now. I want to be a Glam Ma. I want some grandbabies? I can't wait to spoil them."

I went to speak, but my mother cut me off.

"Don't tell me that your career is more important than your biological clock. You're twenty-eight. When you get to thirty, you'll have more complications trying to conceive. Don't end up like your cousin Pita. She is thirty-two and still trying to get pregnant. It's been two years. My sister is going crazy. Don't make me go crazy, Sassy."

I let out an exasperated breath, wondering when she was going to hang up before I ended up hanging up on her. "Yes, mom, you've told me that a million times."

"And when are you going to listen? You know what happened to your cousin Abbie. She messed around and waited until she got old. Then, she snatched up any ole thang. She claims he was the perfect guy. He wasn't perfect if you ask me. He was a bum. I have no idea what she saw in him-"

"Mom!" I interjected.

"Girl, you know I'm telling you the truth. Abbie is old as dirt with a baby on her hip. She's always begging for help. She can't even play with her own baby. Not to mention, she's fat as I don't know what."

"Mama!" I yelled to get her attention.

"What?" my mother asked, annoyed.

"I'm not ready for all that, besides… I…. I don't…" I paused. "I have something to tell you, mom." I was about to come clean and tell her that I was single and I didn't have a man like she always wanted.

"You better not say that you like women. You know I don't play that shit. I expect a marriage and kids from you. I will beat your ass. I want to plan a wedding, be at all of your doctor's appointments, and in the delivery room with all of my grandbabies. Don't deny me of that."

I had to chuckle because my mother wasn't against anyone with an alternative lifestyle. She was just hell bent on controlling my life. She was just old fashion. She wanted my brother and me to be just like her and my father.

"Hee-hee hell. You're over there laughing, but I'm serious. I'm not playing with your ass. You had better have a man in your life. I expect wedding bells soon. "

"I can't with you, mama. Seriously, I'm on the clock."

"Seriously, I don't care. As beautiful as you are and as healthy as you eat with that cute ass shape, long hair, and flawless skin, you had better be courting with a rich young man. Don't bring no broke ass man home either."

"Whatever. I'm about to go."

"Listen, before you do, I called to tell you that Christmas is in Belize this year. Everyone will be there."

"By everyone, do you mean Knox too?"

"Of course, he's family. We're not breaking up with him and his family because you two aren't together anymore. Had you listened to me, you would be married to him already and pregnant with twins."

"I don't care about that. I'm perfectly happy right now," I lied.

"Oh, so you found someone?" my mother beamed. Just hearing the joy in her voice made me happy. That's all I wanted was my mother's approval. "I knew it," she continued without allowing me to get a word in edgewise. "You have to bring him for Christmas."

"No, it's too soon," I said, hoping that she would feel the same about my so-called mystery man. "We've only been dating for six months. I'm not sure where things are going."

"I can't believe you've been holding out on me. I will let your father know that you'll be bringing a plus one."

"But, I-I didn't say that," I stammered.

"Honey, you didn't have to. I know I can be hard on you sometimes. I'm assuming that's why you didn't want your father and me to meet your boyfriend. I promise you that we will not impose all of our family values on your new boyfriend during this trip. I'm just happy that you're dating someone after breaking up with Knox. I had a nightmare that you were alone and throwing yourself into your work to cope. Besides, I'm not sure what tramp your brother will be bringing this year. We definitely went wrong with that boy."

This Thug Love Got Me Trippin: A Belize Christmas

"Listen, mom, I really have to go."

"Call me back later and tell me all about this new boo of yours."

"See, that's why I don't want to bring him. You're already rushing things. Besides, he's spending Christmas with his family," I said, hoping that would change her mind.

"Nonsense. I will see you both in a couple of days. Don't flake out. You know how your father and I feel about Christmas. You had better come. I don't want to hear anything about working overtime or none of that other nonsense that you come up with when you want to get out of family gatherings."

"Okay. I will be there."

"And bring that man of yours too."

"Yes, mom. I'm on the clock. I love you, bye."

I hung up before she could say anything else. I felt a panic attack coming on. I was already stressed out about the made-up boyfriend that I lied to her about. Talking to my mother always brought up anxiety. It was bad enough that I didn't get my dream job at Saxon & Baker. I interned for them and everything and they passed me over for people who graduated with a lower grade point average than I did. There was no doubt in my mind that they were going to hire me because I graduated at the top of my class and I passed the bar on my first try. Practicing law was all I ever dreamed of and it showed because I was a natural.

My last option was being a public defender, which I hated. My clients were all criminals, if you asked me. Almost all of the cases that I looked at proved that they deserved to be in jail. That's why I put the least amount of effort into their cases while I continued to apply for prestigious firms in the city. Of course, I hadn't told my parents that I was a public defender. I was too embarrassed.

"Hi Cassie," my supervisor said cheerfully. The infliction in his voice told me that he wanted something. I could feel it.

"You better not be handing me another case. I'm already swamped," I said while rubbing my temples because I hated this job.

"I'm afraid I have no choice." He sat the folder down on my desk. "Everything is already prepped for you. I wouldn't give this to you, but

This Thug Love Got Me Trippin: A Belize Christmas

Courtney called in sick. Since Christmas is right around the corner, he probably won't be back until after the holiday."

I guessed my supervisor must've known I didn't want to hear his bullshit, so he politely walked away. I thumbed through the folder and sighed. This dude was a real piece of work, starting with his name.

"Did his mama really name him Ace Hood? That's ghetto as hell. What in the world was his mother thinking?"

I frowned as I continued to read the case file. The guy had been arrested for a DUI and he was facing jail time. I had read all I needed to. There wasn't any sense in staying later than what I usually did to prep for his case. Clearly, he was guilty.

Chapter 3

Ace Hood

I sat in jail thinking about all the times that I pushed drugs around the city. I ran in and out of traps without ever getting caught. I mean, I was pushing some serious weight for four years straight and nothing ever happened. I'd never been shot, robbed, or had my life put in jeopardy, period. That's saying a lot, considering I lived in Chicago. Muthafuckas had been shot for way less. One time I saw a nicca get shot over a wing dinner at Harold's. That's just how shit went in the hood.

I was so reckless back then that I didn't even think twice about getting caught. It was as if I was invincible. Driving my fast cars, fucking all types of bad bitches, and blowing money like it grew on trees. You name it and my black ass was doing it. It was a wonder that I graduated with a degree in business. I gave that street life up when I landed a job at Penberly Inc. It was a marketing firm that specialized in product development. And that's where I got the idea for the dog walking app.

It was weird where I came up with the idea. I was at the park one day during my lunch hour and I saw several people walking their dogs. A guy sat down next to me and he went on and on about how he let his ex-girlfriend have his dog when they broke up. Apparently, she was able to care for the dog more. Long story short, he wished that he had someone that he could hire to do all those things that his dog needed while he was at work. Listening to him go on and on about his dog problems birthed my idea for the app.

"Hood!" the guard yelled. "You can get your phone call now."

Slowly, I got off the floor because there wasn't anywhere else to sit. My bones hurt like hell, even though I was only twenty-eight. As bad as I was aching, it felt like I needed to sign up for AARP.

"Hurry up Hood before I change my damn mind. If you don't want to make this call, someone else will be glad to take your place!" the officer barked.

"Sure in the hell would," some wack ass nicca said from the other side of the cell.

"I'm coming, damn," I announced.

I didn't want to say it too loud. I needed my phone call. Following behind the guard, I walked up to the phone and picked it up while he carried on a conversation. The person I dialed was my cousin Cakes because he would get me out of this shit asap, but the phone just rang. I called my boys and none of them niccas picked up either. They were probably all passed out somewhere or knee-deep in some pussy. I called the last person I ever wanted to call, my mother. Of course, she answered on the first ring.

"Where are you? I've been worried sick."

"Um, I had a little situation."

I heard my mother suck her teeth and I could only imagine her expression. "What kind of situation?"

I wanted to beat around the bush, but I couldn't; I was on a time limit. "Probably your worst nightmare."

I heard her gasp before I continued.

"I'm in jail."

"Boy, you had better be lying," my mother scoffed.

"I wish I was, ma. I got arrested on a DUI. Are you going to get me out?"

"Listen, I don't have any money."

"What about dad? Does he have it?"

"No, we're living from check to check. We barely have anything. Besides, I told you this shit was going to happen."

"I don't need your lecture right now, ma. Not when I'm locked up."

"Son, I love you, and I will give you the world. But, I can't baby you anymore. The cord was cut when you moved out on your own. At some point, you have to grow up, make your own mistakes, and pay for them."

Click!

I heard my mother sobbing before she hung up.

"Ma!" The line was dead.

"Your time is up, Hood." The officer grabbed me by my arm and ushered me back towards the crowded cell.

"What about a lawyer? I want a lawyer."

"Do you have one?"

I was stunned. Not only did I not have a lawyer, I didn't have a pot to piss in, a window to throw it out of, the grass for it to land on, or the fertilizer to keep the grass green. A nicca was hella fucked.

"No, I don't," I mumbled, embarrassed.

"Then, you'll get a court appointed one just like all the rest of the losers."

With that being said, he shoved me back into the cell with a bunch of homeless people and a few criminals that looked as if they wanted to fight the world. It was the weekend, so I knew I was going to be fucked until Monday. I copped a squat back in the pissy corner that I was in previously and pulled my jacket over my head. I'm sure the van would be coming to process us soon, since I wasn't leaving.

I was so angry at myself. I went to Loyola and graduated with a degree in Business Administration. I was working on my MBA when I lost my job. I was such a loser. I couldn't be mad at my mother for leaving me in here. I'd thrown my whole life away for a piece of thot pussy and several drinks.

*****

I walked into the courtroom wearing a jumpsuit and chains. All eyes were on me as I walked to the front. Since I couldn't afford a lawyer, I assumed they appointed one for me. I just hoped it wasn't a shitty ass public defender who thought all his or her clients were guilty because we were poor.

As I was being escorted to the front of the courtroom, in front of the judge, I caught the look of the stuck-up woman who was representing me. I knew a stuck-up ass muthafucka when I saw one. She looked like a real live bitch. Someone who needed some dick in her life. The nasty look on her face told me that she was aggravated with the world and she was going to take all of her frustrations out on my case. I sat down next to her, and she frowned at me as if I were a piece of trash.

"Are you ready, Miss Treyton?" the judge asked with an impatient look on her face.

"I motion for a continuation, your honor. I just got the case last night and I'm not fully prepared."

"And why not?" Judge Bonner asked.

"Because my colleague called out sick and I was stuck presenting this case today. I haven't even had a chance to meet with my client because I've been in court with other clients all morning."

The judge pulled her glasses down to her nose, looking over them at us. "And whose fault is that?"

My lawyer frowned even more. "The city, your honor. How am I supposed to represent clients when we are under staffed and overworked? I petition for a raise and a new budget that can afford more public defenders."

The judge laughed uncontrollably and I just knew I was fucked then. Her laugh was loud and cynical. Anyone with ears could tell that she was about to clap back. However, my lawyer must not have gotten the memo. She was going on and on about what she wouldn't do and how she wasn't appreciated.

"Order in the court, Miss Treyton!" the judge yelled, banging her gavel. "You have a lot of nerve. I'm going to give you a pass because I can tell you are new and this is your first day in my court. But, let me make one thing clear, nobody twisted your arm to become a lawyer and serve the public. You could have easily took up another profession. However, if you're going to stand in my courtroom and represent anyone, I believe that you need to humble yourself and service the client. Otherwise, you're wasting this young man's time as well as mine."

My lawyer sighed and rolled her eyes to the sky. "Yes, your honor."

The judge shuffled through a few papers and then she asked how do you plead?

My lawyer smiled and confidently said, "Guilty, your honor. My client admits to all charges."

"Bullshit!" I hollered. "I ain't never admitted to shit. Where did you get that from? I'm not guilty."

"So, you're saying that you weren't drunk the night that you were arrested?" this stuck-up ass bitch had the nerve to ask me.

"What did you say, bitch?" I barked.

"I asked you a question," she replied boldly.

"Were you drunk or not? Because I have the toxicology report and it says your blood alcohol level was through the roof."

The judge banged the gavel. "Order in the court."

"Bitch, you're fired!" I barked. "Obviously, you don't care about nobody but yourself. I'm better off defending myself. I want a new lawyer," I expressed to the judge. "She's cracked like a sidewalk. I refuse to be represented by someone like her."

"Order in the court," the judge said again, banging her gavel, but neither one of us listened.

"You can't fire me," Miss Treyton stated. "You ought to be glad that someone is representing your broke ass."

"Hold up, you don't know me," I flexed. "I'll beat your ass."

"Do it then."

I was about to literally square up with my lawyer when two officers handcuffed us, restraining us both. We were ushered out of the courtroom into the judge's chambers. She was sitting before us as we stood.

"What's going on here?" Judge Bonner

asked us with a frustrated look on her face. "Is this a relationship gone bad, or are you two in love but afraid to admit it?"

I was highly offended because I would never fuck with a chick like this. She might have been a great lawyer on paper, but she sucked in person.

"Listen, your honor," I started. "I apologize for my behavior, but I never met this chick a day in my life. She approached me wrong and I fired back. That's all there is to it. As she stated, she's filling in for someone. If you can find it in your heart to continue the case until another lawyer can represent me, I would appreciate it.

The judge sighed. "Against my better judgement, I'm going to postpone this hearing until after Christmas. I hope you can find better legal counsel by then."

"Thank you, judge. What about bail?"

"I'm going to allow you to leave today on your word."

"Thank you, your honor."

"Don't thank me too fast. I expect you to be in court on December 27th. I'm only allowing you to leave because you do not have any priors. However, that doesn't mean I won't find you guilty when you come back and throw your butt in jail. I'm giving you a break because everyone deserves proper legal representation." Judge Bonner's eyes landed on Miss Treyton. It looked as if she wanted to throw up.

My fake ass lawyer looked over at me and rolled her eyes so hard, I thought they were going to fall out of her head. She acted like I was the one at fault, when she was the one who just showed her ass in court.

"And you, young lady, you'd better get your act together before I petition for you to be disbarred. Your behavior was a disgrace today in my courtroom and a disgrace to the justice system."

"Yes, your honor," she mumbled. "It won't happen again.

"I have a headache after this charade. You're both dismissed." Judge Bonner waved us both away like flies.

I was escorted in one direction and my fake ass lawyer was escorted in another. I hoped like hell I'd never see her snooty ass ever again.

Chapter 4

Cassie "Sassy" Treyton

That nicca Ace Hood's name was etched in my damn brain. I hated him. He almost got me fired with his ghetto ass. I didn't understand why he couldn't just take the guilty plea. He knew damn well he was driving while under the influence. I couldn't stand people like that who didn't want to take responsibility for their behavior. That's what was wrong with society right now. Everyone wanted to do what they wanted to do with no consequences.

Now, my career was in the toilet. Judge Bonner was cool with my mentor, so I was sure to hear about my poor behavior in the courtroom. My disdain for my job spilled over into the courtroom and I humiliated myself. The judged hated me and she was probably going to ruin my reputation before I could get started.

I walked into my house and went straight to the fridge and got the bottle of wine that was chilled. I needed it. I considered getting a wine glass but decided to guzzle from the bottle, taking it to the head. After drinking nearly half the bottle, I sat down at my kitchen table with my Olive Garden salad and fettuccine Alfredo. I stabbed at my salad, suddenly losing my appetite when my phone rang.

"Hello," I answered.

"Bitch, you better open this door. I've been ringing this doorbell since forever. It's chilly and I don't want my skin to get too ashy."

I laughed despite my sour mood and ran to the front door to open it. On my porch stood my two best friends: Reesha & Cakes. I opened the door and let them both in before I sauntered back into the kitchen. Cakes took one look at the wine bottle I was holding and shook his head.

"Reesha said it was bad, but I had no idea it was this bad. You're drinking out of whole bottles, bitch?" Cakes dramatically put one hand to his forehead as if he was praying for me before he spoke again. "Okay, so you had a bad first day in court. Suck that shit up, bitch."

Reesha had a little more empathy as she sat down next to me with a pouty face. "Tell me what's wrong?"

I sat the wine bottle down and burst into tears. "Everything," I sobbed. "I got into it with my client in court. He was guilty and he had the nerve to be arrogant."

Cakes laughed. "I bet you told him that he was guilty, didn't you?"

I nodded my head, wiping away my tears. Reesha hugged me tighter.

Cakes tossed his hands in the air dramatically. "Your damn mouth is always counting checks your ass can't cash. I don't know what you'd do without your besties."

"That's right, Sassy." Reesha was wiping away my tears like a big sister. "Despite Cakes' snide remarks, we are here for you always. You know that right?"

I sniffed and nodded my head. "My life is over. Not only is my career in a downward spiral, I lied and told my mother I would bring my boyfriend for our Christmas vacation."

Cakes spit out the water he was drinking. "Bitch, have you lost your mind? You don't have a damn man. Why would you lie to your mother like that?"

The serious look on his face made Reesha and I crack up. He all bent out of shape and it wasn't even his problem.

I huffed loudly and told my friends the truth. "I told my mother that I had a boyfriend. Well, technically, she assumed it and I just let her keep assuming. I never thought she would invite him to our family Christmas gathering. I just wanted my mother to back off and stop grilling me about my love life. Knox is going to be there too. So, not only do I have to face my parents grilling me about my love life, I have to see my ex-boyfriend who dumped me last Christmas."

The pity that they both displayed on their faces made me want to crawl under the table and die a slow death. I felt so stupid. I should have never gone along with the fabricated story. I was mad at myself for being in such a stupid predicament.

"I'm going to tell my mother the truth."

This Thug Love Got Me Trippin: A Belize Christmas

"Wait a minute, bitch. Let me think, damn."

Reesha and I watched Cakes as he dramatically thought of an answer to my problem.

"I think I might be able to help you out. What about a fake boyfriend?" He smiled and raised his eyebrows, indicating that he'd come up with a master plan.

"That's a good idea," Reesha chimed in. "Then, you could save face in front of your parents and get your ex-boyfriend back."

"I'm not sure if I want Knox back."

Reesha eyed me. "Girl, boo. As much as you talk about Knox, you definitely want him back and this fake boyfriend will definitely get your man back. He'll go crazy when he finds out you got someone else and you're not moping around about his ass."

"You both make great points. The only problem is I don't have a fake boyfriend. Hell, if I could get a fake one, I might have been able to get a real one."

Cakes laughed. "That's why your gay bestie is going to hook you up. I got the perfect guy."

"I can't bring a gay dude home, Cakes. I would never hear the end of it. Then, I'd be subjected to her hooking me up with another one of her friend's sons. Been there, done that."

Cakes ran his fingers under the water spout and sprinkled me with water. "Stop being funny. The guy I'm thinking about is not gay. He's my cousin in fact and he loves women. I think he'd be perfect for your fake boyfriend. He's smart, educated, and handsome."

"What cousin is this?" Reesha asked. "Most of your cousins are a mess."

Cakes rolled his eyes to the ceiling. "That might be true, but you haven't met this cousin. He's been preoccupied lately. We're just now catching up. He's a good guy. We're more like brothers since his parents took me in when my parents died. When kids used to tease me at school for being different, he always fought for me."

"Sounds like a really great guy," Reesha exclaimed.

"He is. I know what you like," Cakes said, pointing to me. "And I know what type of guy would impress your parents. You trust me or nah?"

I sighed. "I don't know, Cakes. My parents

can be brutal, especially my mom. She can sniff out bullshit a mile away."

"Honey, I wouldn't even be offering this solution if I didn't think it would work. Have I ever let you down?"

I smiled. "No, you haven't. So, run this by me again."

"I thought you'd never ask. You're going to use my cousin to get your boo back."

I just shook my head with a grin. "But, I said I didn't want him back."

Cakes and Reesha looked at each other and laughed as if I was a joke.

"We both know that's not true," Reesha commented.

"Like I said before," Cakes stated. "He's handsome. Definitely your type and the perfect man to make your ex boo jealous. He's the perfect beau to parade around in front of your family."

"If he's that cute, why is he single?"

"He's focused on his career," Cakes replied.

I gave him a skeptical look. "And what does he do exactly?"

"He has a degree in marketing, but he's

always been very smart since I can remember."

Reesha frowned up her face. "You keep saying how handsome and smart he is, but what about his swag? He can't be no lame."

"You mean like Knox?" Cakes replied. "He's the epitome of boring, chile."

"Yes, he is, but I can't help who I love."

Reesha and Knox both gasped.

"You finally admit it," Cakes exclaimed. "Love is in the air for Christmas."

I wanted my ex back because I felt like he was the one that got away. He dumped me because I chose my career over being a wife and motherhood. Now that I'm a lawyer, I feel like I made a huge mistake. I wanted the family that every woman dreamed of and I felt like I could have that with Knox. Being a lawyer was my dream, but it wasn't worth losing my relationship and the chance to have my own family. During the Christmas vacation, I planned on expressing how much I missed and loved Knox. That our break up was my fault and I planned on giving my career up and being a stay at home wife and mother like he wanted. Knox was very well established, so money wasn't an object. He would provide for me and the kids with no problem.

"I'm glad you finally came around and admitted to still loving Knox. That shit was like pulling teeth." Cakes went into my fridge to see what I had to eat. "Why is your fridge always empty? See, this is why you can't keep a man. Your ass ain't never prepared to cook nothing." He folded his top lip up to his nose to emphasize his disgust.

"Whatever. If everything goes right, I'll have a maid and a cook," I firmly stated. "Tell your cousin that I'm willing to pay him five thousand dollars for doing this favor for me."

"Five thousand?" both of my besties exclaimed.

"Shit, I'd be your straight boyfriend for that amount."

I laughed loudly, feeling much better. The tears had stopped flowing and I felt much better about seeing my parents. I hugged Cakes and Reesha, kissing them both on the cheek. We shared another bottle of wine before Cakes left to go speak to his cousin.

Chapter 5

Ace Hood

I thought that the day I lost my job was the worst day of my life. Then, the worst was when my fiancée walked out of my life. Clearly, I was wrong. I'd reached an all-time low when my damn lawyer couldn't defend me because she thought I was guilty. What kinda shackle hang a nicca, slave-trade mentality did that broad have?

I knew she was going to be a super bitch when she started filing her damn nails in the courtroom. I assumed it was because she was trying to use some tactic on the defense. Honestly, I was not sure what I thought. Her behavior was strange before she represented me. I just thought maybe she would get her shit together before talked to the judge on my behalf.

This Thug Love Got Me Trippin: A Belize Christmas

Boy, was I wrong. This bitch was a real nutcase.

"Are you listening to me, son?" my father spat. "How long are you going to throw your life away?"

"Dad, I'm not. I made one mistake. Sometimes, things happen out of my control. I'm not perfect."

My father snorted and banged on the table. "What you did was serious. I'm tired of you downplaying what's really going on in your life. You're out of control. When are you going to admit it to yourself and live in your truth?"

"Your father's right, you know?" my mother agreed. "We've been watching you mess your life up since you lost your job. You don't have to let life get the best of you. Plenty of people have fell on hard times and bounced back."

"That's what I'm trying to do. I didn't do any of this on purpose. The way you two make it sound, I am just a royal fuck up."

My father jumped up from the table and tried to beat the snot out of me. I was faster than my old man, racing upstairs until I got to my room, locking the door swiftly.

"I'm going to beat your ass as soon as you

come out," my father scolded.

I flipped the bird at the door and flopped down on my twin-sized bed. I wanted to piss him off like he'd pissed me off. I had to get my shit in order because I didn't know how much longer I could stay with my parents. I was sure I was on their nerves, but they were on mine as well. Most of our arguments had to do with my financial issues. They were tired of helping me out and I was sick of the shit too. I wanted my own money and my crib back. Staying in my old room was cramping my style. It was hard as fuck trying to convince a girl to give up some pussy on a twin bed.

My parents had no idea what I was going through. They'd been married since the dinosaurs walked the earth. What did they know about heartache? My father had been on his job for eons, and my mother worked whenever she felt like it. Neither one of them knew what it was like to lose a job. They'd been in this house since I was born. Once again, they'd never experienced homelessness. My point was my parents couldn't understand any parts of my predicament or how I felt. They were being judgmental and insensitive to my feelings.

It's crazy because Christmas was in two days and it didn't even feel like it. If I hadn't seen the tree decorated in the living room, I would have forgotten all about the holiday. Shit had been so bad that I wasn't even looking forward to Christmas.

Knock. Knock. Knock.

"Who is it?" I barked. I just knew it was my mother or father coming to finish me off.

"Cakes," he replied in a sweet voice.

I knew it was him because nobody I knew could imitate that voice. It had to be my cousin. I cracked the door, peeping through to make sure it was him before I allowed him to come in.

"Nicca, you looking like you're hiding from the Feds," Cakes replied as he walked inside of my bedroom.

"Nah, nothing like that. Moms and pops tripping hard. They stay riding my ass about everything."

"Well, I know someone who could help you out?"

"Yeah. Who is that?" I asked, flopping down back on my bed with a blunt in my hand.

"You want a hit?"

"I'll pass. I'm here to help out my bestie."

I lit my blunt and started smoking, calming my nerves immediately. "Yeah. What kinda help?"

"She needs a man in her life."

"Shit, what bitch doesn't?" I questioned with a cough from this strong ass weed. "That's what every woman I know wants."

"No, you don't understand," Cakes exclaimed. "She's willing to pay."

My ears perked up immediately. "How much?"

"Five stacks."

"Word? Is she a dog or sum?" I inquired, wondering if she was butt ugly. "I'm not fucking no ugly bitch. I'm hard up for cash, but not that hard up. Fuck that."

"No. It's nothing like that," Cakes reassured. "She's actually beautiful and she comes from a well-to-do family. She's been so focused on her career that she hasn't had time to date. Her parents invited her on a Christmas vacation where her old boo would be there. She wants to make him jealous so he will take her back."

This Thug Love Got Me Trippin: A Belize Christmas

"Okay, what does that have to do with me?" I asked, blowing out smoke rings.

"Everything, jackass. She's paying five thousand. I brought this to you since you could use the money."

I sat up on the bed so fast, it made my head spin and I started choking. "How much did you say?"

"I said my bestie is willing to pay you five thousand to be her fake boyfriend for Christmas."

"Damn, she got bread like that to throw away?"

Cakes shrugged. "She comes from a pretty wealthy family. Five thousand is chump change for her."

I hit the blunt again and thought for a minute. "Hmmmm. Chump change, huh? Well, make it ten racks then."

Cakes looked at me and shook his head. "Are you serious?"

"You muthafuckin' right I am. She needs a nicca for Christmas and I need the bread. She got what I want and I got what she wants. It's a fair trade if you ask me."

Cakes exhaled loudly, followed by a

disgusting groan. "Ugh, you make me sick as hell. Let me text her and see if she'll go for it."

I sat on my bed smoking my blunt while Cakes texted his bestie. He looked up at me a few times while he texted. I was not sure why but, if baby girl wasn't giving up ten, she could kiss her fake ass boyfriend goodbye. I was hard up for the money, but not that damn hard up. She was going to pay me to be a damn actor.

"Do you have a passport?" Cakes asked me out the blue.

I didn't understand what that had to do with my money, but I answered his question anyway. "Yes. Why?"

He ignored me and went back to texting.

This secretive shit was getting on my nerves. "Is she in or not, man?"

"She's in," he finally said. "You better not take her money and skip town either."

"Nicca, I ain't never did no shit like that. I'm a man of my word. You should know that shit. If I said I'ma do it, I'ma do it. Just tell her I want five stacks up front and the other half once our Christmas relationship is over."

Cakes texted that to her and replied, "Cool."

This Thug Love Got Me Trippin: A Belize Christmas

"So, why did she want to know if I had a passport?"

"Because her family is having Christmas in Belize."

"Word? Oh, they balling out of control I see."

"Something like that. She said be at the airport at six am. She texted me all of the flight information and I'ma text it to you now. She'll be there waiting for you at check in."

My phone chimed and I looked at the text that Cakes sent me. We were flying first class. I was glad I did hit this chick up for more money. She was loaded.

Chapter 6

Cassie "Sassy" Treyton

It was Christmas Eve morning and I couldn't wait to get this tirade over with. We had a four-hour flight and I planned on sleeping the whole way. I hoped my mother was happy. I was doing all this extra shit to please her. Hearing her mouth for the next couple of days would have drove me half crazy. I'd rather bribe some dude I didn't know to be in a pretend relationship than to suffer a million questions from my mother.

I arrived at the airport a little earlier. I wanted to make sure that I saw this nicca before he saw me. I didn't get his name or what he looked like. All I had was Cakes' word and the five thousand dollars in an envelope waiting for my mystery man. My eyes continued to scan the airport, waiting for his cousin to arrive. The airport was starting to get crowded. Each guy that passed by, I wondered if that was him. Anxiety was starting to kick in and I wished that I had asked Cakes for a picture of his cousin. At the time, I was just thankful that I had someone to fill in at such a short notice.

When I saw that the time was ten past six, I started to get impatient. Where was this dude at? I stood there checking my Rolex every second. Cakes said he was handsome and physically fit, so I kept looking at all the black young men who fit the description of Cakes' cousin. Airport traffic was really starting to pour in and people were coming at me in every direction. As I scurried to get out of the way, someone bumped into me. I mean, they hit my ass so hard that I fell backwards on my ass.

"Sorry, shorty, let me help you up," a smooth and sultry voice said.

I was a little dazed, but I could have sworn his voice sounded familiar. I reached out my arm to him while trying to get my bearings. He helped me up and that's when I got a good look at him. He had on a designer hoodie and joggers, but he was still the same guilty thug that I defended in court yesterday.

"Get your hands off me!" I shouted, snatching my hand away from this thug.

Ace took a step back and stared at me for a moment as if he was trying to place my face. His eyes lit up and then they turned to slits when he recognized me. "Aww, hell naw. What are you doing here?"

I dusted off my bottom. "Last time I checked, thug, your name isn't on the airport. If you bought it since I saw you yesterday, then you could afford to hire yourself a lawyer instead of wasting taxpayer's money."

"Naw, what you should have said was I would be able to hire me a real lawyer instead of a pretend one like your fake bougie ass. Obviously, the government is hiring anyone nowadays. I should apply too. Maybe I could defend you after you get your license revoked."

"No thanks to your black ass. You almost got me fired."

"You should have been. You didn't defend me or any other client that you had. How could you call yourself a public defender when you didn't defend shit?"

"Your mama didn't defend shit," I spat.

"And your daddy birthed a piece of shit," he clapped back.

I rolled up my sleeves and balled up my fists, ready to fight. "Listen, I've had enough of your smart ass mouth."

"Same here. It ain't nothing but space and opportunity."

We were both squaring up, about to punch each other's lights out, when there was a call announcing the flight to Belize. We both stopped arguing and looked up at the terminal board.

"I don't have time to be arguing with you. This is my flight and I'm here meeting someone to board for a great Christmas in Belize."

Ace stared at me real funny. "Wait a minute? You're going to Belize?"

"Yeah, why?"

"I'm going to Belize too."

Now, it was my turn to stare at him. Everything was starting to make sense now. "This can't be happening," I said more to myself than him. "Please don't tell me you're Cakes' cousin."

Princess Diamond

Ace's low bedroom eyes widened with surprise. "Bruh, please tell me you're not the chick who needed a fake boyfriend for Christmas?"

I shushed him. "Would you lower your damn voice? If I wanted the whole airport to know, I would have announced it over the speaker."

"Listen, I know you're not pleased with this situation. I damn sure ain't either. But, I'ma keep it real, shorty; you need a nicca on your arm and I need the bread. As much as it pains me to spend a few days with your bougie ass, I'm willing to do so for ten G's. So, what's it going to be? Are you in or not?"

I was utterly disgusted as I listened to our flight being announced again. Literally, I had no time to think this over. It was time to check in or turn around. We needed to get through airport security and make our way to the gate before it was too late. I closed my eyes and contemplated what to do next. Should I deal with this thug or not? I sighed a million times before I answered him.

"Fine. You got a deal."

This Thug Love Got Me Trippin: A Belize Christmas

I had no choice but to deal with him, even though I didn't want to. He was my only hope. I was going to kill Cakes when I returned.

"Cool. Hand me my money and off we go."

I pulled the sealed envelope out of my inner jacket pocket and handed it to him. "Here. Now, let's get this relationship started, boyfriend."

He side eyed me and handed his license to the man at the counter. I made sure to get a double look, just to make sure his name was really Ace Hood. It was. Ugh. So ghetto. I handed my license to the man as well and our tickets were printed. We both put our luggage on the belt and it was whisked away.

Neither one of us said a word as we went through airport security. He was much more prepared than me because he had his shoes and hoodie off and everything extra in the bins as directed. I struggled. I had on tons of jewelry and all kinds of extra shit that kept making the scanner beep until they decided to search me.

Ace stood off to the side on his phone, as if he didn't give a shit about me being felt up and searched. I swear it felt like the man searching me was trying to stick his fingers in my coochie. I was positive that he squeezed my ass a few times while he pretended to be professional. It wasn't nothing professional about that gold-tooth asshole. When the whole situation was over and done with, I felt violated as we made our way to our boarding gate. I struggled with my carry-on while Ace strolled ahead of me with his bag securely on his back. Once we found a joining seat, I plopped my bag down next to him.

"Can you watch my bag?"

He pulled out his Bluetooth earbuds. "Don't take too long."

"I'll be right back."

"Aight."

I stared at him as he settled in his seat with his eyes closed and his hood over his head. He better not let my Louis Vuitton carryon get stolen. I know that much. Reaching into my handbag, I pulled out my phone and walked far away from our terminal so that I could talk freely.

"Bitch, I ought to beat your ass."

"What's wrong?" Cakes inquired.

"Your cousin is the thug nicca that I had to represent in court. The guilty nicca that I complained to you about yesterday."

This Thug Love Got Me Trippin: A Belize Christmas

Cakes gasped. "I had no idea. He didn't mention anything about getting locked up."

"Well, he did. He was arrested for a DUI. Your thug cousin almost got me disbarred. Now, I have to spend the next couple days with his ass pretending to be in love and shit."

Cakes gasped again. "Gurl, I'm truly sorry. I had no idea. I wouldn't have suggested him if I knew y'all already had beef. So, what you gone do, bitch?"

"The fuck you think I'm going to do? I paid his ass the money and told him he had better act his ass off. It's too late to find someone else. The plane is about to board."

"I know you about to have some piping hot T when you come back."

I groaned. "Your ass owes me. I want a fabulous Christmas gift when I return.

"I got you, boo. I owe you big time after this fuck up."

"Yes, the hell you do. I want maid service from you for a week."

Cakes giggled. "You got it, boo. Whatever it takes so that you don't stay mad at me. Now, go have fun and don't kill my cousin. It's only two days. You can do it."

"I'ma try not to. He's already worked my last nerve."

We made kissy sounds to each other before I hung up. I checked Ace out as I approached him. Yesterday when I was forced to defend him, I really didn't pay attention to how sexy he was. There was no denying his thug appeal. He was extremely attractive. His slender toned body, smooth vanilla skin, sea-sick waves, sexy bedroom eyes, and that dick print. I tried not to notice while we were arguing, but I saw that big muthafucka flexing on his thigh. His cologne had me going crazy. It was my favorite scent and quite expensive for a dude who had to retain free legal counsel.

"What?" he asked when he caught me staring. He looked at me like I had the plague.

I cleared my throat and recovered quickly. "Um, I forgot to give you the notebook with all of the details of my boyfriend."

"Say what?" Ace asked, sitting up. He looked me up and down with a sexy frown.

This Thug Love Got Me Trippin: A Belize Christmas

I wasn't sure why I was associating him with sex now. That had me weirded out. Why was I attracted to him all of a sudden?

"I made a notebook for you with all the details that you have to memorize in order to be my fake boyfriend."

Chapter 7

Ace Hood

This bitch was tripping. I snatched the thick notebook out of her hand and skimmed though it. "Yo, are you serious? This shit looks like a thesis."

"It's detailed," she exclaimed with an attitude.

She was so clueless. I found myself chuckling so that I didn't cuss her ass out. Who does that? Hand writes all the answers and questions for a pretend boyfriend. This chick was sick as fuck. Definitely a coo-coo bird. I was starting to question if the money was really worth it. Was she gonna get me to Belize and kidnap my ass? I mean, from what she had displayed over the last twenty-four hours, anything was possible.

This Thug Love Got Me Trippin: A Belize Christmas

"Ay, I'm not about to memorize this shit. You got me hella fucked up."

Before she could reach for the notebook, I tossed the shit in the large trash can nearby. She shrieked and looked down the long barrel before she stared at me with hatred.

"You asshole. You threw our relationship in the trash," she exclaimed, reaching her hand into the dirty bin, trying to regain the information.

It was at this point when I understood why she needed to pay for a man. Her priorities were all fucked up. She wanted to build a nicca. That's not how shit worked in the real world. Then again, she was a rich princess who got her way. Well, not today. I wasn't about to feed off into that pompous bullshit, no matter how much she paid me. She wanted a good performance and I intended on giving her money's worth. That didn't mean I had to turn into a robotic boyfriend with memorized quotes. Fuck outta here.

This chick was crazy on top of being a liar. None of this shit made any sense. There was no way I was going to remember all the shit she had listed. I would be the biggest fool ever if I even thought about doing that shit.

With an attitude, Cassie returned to her seat. "I hope that you read some of that shit. It took me hours to create that notebook."

"Yeah, I glanced the shit over, but that's not the move. I can't be the person you need me to be with a bunch of memorized bullshit."

"So, what are you going to do? Be yourself?"

"Yeah, why not. That's the best way to convince someone. Be true and the rest will follow. I will stretch the truth a little since you did pay me; be clear, that shit ain't in my DNA."

"So, you think you got this?" she quizzed.

"No doubt. I always got it."

"Not always. But, anyway, let me test you then?"

Ace waved his hand at me. "Nah. Not gonna happen."

"Why not? I need to make sure you're prepared for my parents. They can be brutal."

"I got this. They gone love me. You just worry about you and all the bullshit ass lies you told them because I'm not about to entertain that. You look like the type to lay out a whole bunch of lies to save face."

This Thug Love Got Me Trippin: A Belize Christmas

I pouted. "I don't." He was right, but I refused to tell him so.

"I see you're in denial too."

Out of nowhere, she started giggling like a crazy woman.

"What's so funny?"

"Are you going to keep your real name?"

I was offended. "Yeah, why? What's wrong with my name?"

She laughed even harder. "It represents every stereotype that I can think of. I would recommend you use the name that I had in the notebook. It'll save you the embarrassment."

"You might be afraid of your parents, but I'm not. I love my name. I was named after my father and he was named after his father. My name has legacy, something bougie ass black folks don't seem to know nothing about. Who the fuck has Christmas in Belize anyway? It ain't even no damn snow."

My comment stopped her ass from laughing immediately. Her mouth hung open and I was sure she felt stupid as hell.

"Now that I finally got your attention without your mouth flapping a mile a minute, this is how this is going to work. I'ma say what the fuck I want and how the fuck I want to say it, or I can walk away now and keep the five stacks."

She gasped again, holding her chest as if I'd spit on her or something. "Oh no, you won't keep my money if you're not going to Belize."

I walked up on her so that she knew I meant business. "I said I'ma keep the shit. The way I see it, your ass owes me anyway because you nearly got me thrown in jail for some bullshit."

"You-you were guilty," she stuttered.

We stood there staring at each other. I was sure to the average eye we looked as if we were deep in love looking into each other's eyes. However, if they looked closely, they would see the fire in her eyes and the darts in mine.

Being this close to her, I finally noticed how pretty she was. I mean, she wasn't just a pretty girl, she was drop-dead gorgeous with a cute little frame. Small perky breasts, hazel eyes, long eyelashes, and long dark hair. Even in her Victoria Secret Pink leggings and tunic, her ass was looking soft and round.

"Why are you looking at me like that?"

This Thug Love Got Me Trippin: A Belize Christmas

I wiped drool from my lip and snapped out of my trance. For a minute, I forgot that she was my enemy. I walked up on her even more, towering over her. For the first time, she looked intimidated.

"Forget it. It's whatever. I can't deal with you any longer. You win."

Cassie sauntered over to the seats, flopping down with a pout. Her bottom lip was poked out so far that it looked like it was going to fall off her face and hit the floor. I wanted to laugh, but she definitely looked really cute with her pouty lip. A part of me wanted to scoop her into my arms and kiss her sexy little ass.

It didn't make no sense how spoiled she was. That was her real problem. She acted like a bitch because she was used to getting her way. When I rebelled against her, she submitted to me. I ain't never encountered no chick like her before. She was irrational and didn't make any damn sense most of the time, yet I was intrigued by her and my dick was starting to swell. It was as if what pissed me off turned me on at the same time. I guess there was a thin line between love and hate.

Princess Diamond

I sat next to Cassie with a smirk on my face, and she got up and scooted one seat over. She looked as if she wanted to punch me in the face. I couldn't hold back the laugh that escaped. Her childish ways were annoying but kinda cute at the same time. It was time for me to turn up the heat on Miss Treyton a little more.

"I'm not going to your family Christmas holiday extravaganza."

"Why not?" she asked, all freaked out.

I wanted to laugh so badly, but I knew that she would have figured out that I was joking. "I'm not feeling you or this. I'ma take my money and be out."

"No," she begged, moving back into the seat next to me. "You have to come. I've already told my family about you."

"Oh really. Did you tell everyone about me or did you tell everyone about Rudolph?"

Cassie's pretty mouth formed a sexy O before she rolled her eyes.

"You wanted me to be named Rudolph instead of Ace? C'mon, shorty. That name was lame as fuck. Ain't no way my parents would have named me that shit."

This Thug Love Got Me Trippin: A Belize Christmas

I threw my hands in the air dramatically with a smirk.

Cassie sighed. "Okay, you might raise a good point. Rudolph is a little lame."

She smiled and I smiled too.

She put her hand on mine. "I promise to back off a little if you decide to stay. However, the choice is totally up to you, but I hope you change your mind. I really need your help."

"Are you begging?"

She cut her eyes at me. "Don't push it, Ace. I still think you're a thug."

Chapter 8

Cassie "Sassy" Treyton

We were finally on the plane and all I could think about was how he threw away my thesis, as he called it. It took me all night to think of all those details. Then, he had the nerve to be mad at me. Hell, he was the unreasonable one. He was going to ditch my ass as soon as we got there.

I was going to be so embarrassed if Ace flew all the way to Belize, and then he decided to get his shit and bounce. That had to be the worst. Having a supposed to be boyfriend stand me up would suck. I had to do something to stop him, but what would that be? I wasn't used to dudes like him. I was used to men who were head over heels for me and they let me get my way.

This Thug Love Got Me Trippin: A Belize Christmas

The last guy who gave me an ultimatum was my ex, Knox. That's probably the reason why I was on a plane with a fake ass boyfriend who I paid to spend Christmas with me and my family. Nervousness kicked in. I just hoped that Ace made Knox jealous, so Knox would take me back. I was lonely and I was tired of using a massager to get the job done late at night.

I looked over at Ace, who was bobbing his head to the music in his earbuds. I didn't understand why Ace couldn't just do like I said. Why couldn't he just memorize the damn instructions that I laid out for him and play along? Shit, ain't that why I paid his ass. For goodness sakes, he was here for me. He was my fake boyfriend, which meant he should be doing what I said.

I glared at his ass and he smirked. That damn smirk was sexy. I sighed while still side-eyeing him. I was a nervous damn wreck and Ace was cool as a fan. He ordered him a couple of drinks while watching some video on his phone. Every time he laughed, I wanted to scream. Finally, I just pulled out my tablet and began reading a law journal.

Princess Diamond

While I was reading, Ace's head slumped over in my lap. At first, I thought his ass was trying to be funny. I was about to knock him into next week when I realized he was sleep. He done drank up half the bar and now this nicca was in a drunken state, sprawled across my damn lap. I couldn't believe his drunk ass just fell into my lap. He had the nerve to wrap his arms around my waist, curling even closer to me. Cakes sure knew how to pick them.

I groaned and placed my tablet on his head. I didn't want him touching me at first until the warmth of his body excited me. My mind was annoyed as fuck, but my body was super aroused. My pussy was juicy because his face was so close. Everything about this man screamed run, but my body wasn't going to let me. I tried to concentrate on reading, but now the only thing that filled my head was sex thoughts. I noticed his dick print a long time ago and now that we'd made body contact, I was ready to know what he was working with. Ugh. I hated my pussy. If I didn't watch it, she was going to have me fucking Ace instead of Knox.

This Thug Love Got Me Trippin: A Belize Christmas

I checked him out while he slept. I even ran my hand across his smooth face, admiring him as he slept. He was really a cutie. Maybe if he wasn't such an asshole and his life was better together, I might have given him a chance. As fast as that thought popped into my mind, I tried to blink it away. Knox was the man for me, not Ace. Although, I couldn't help but imagine how it would be to have him as my real boyfriend.

*****

I didn't even know that I had drifted off to sleep until I heard the captain's voice. He was announcing that we were about to land. I gave Ace a hard shove and he sprung up from my lap, staring at me crazy.

"Don't push me like that again."

Now, it was my turn to smile and smirk at him. He stretched and I could see his dick through his joggers. It was leaning on his thigh like a snake. Lawd, this man was so sexy. I had to repent in my head to stay focused because none of this was real.

"Excuse me, but I need you to get back into your seat and buckle up," the flight attendant told Ace.

He grimaced at her, but he sat back down and put his seatbelt on like she asked.

"Stop checking me out!" he barked.

I had finally gotten back into my law journal when he made that outburst. "What are you talking about?" I snapped.

"You know what I'm talking about."

"No, I don't, and I don't appreciate you accusing me of anything."

"So, I'm accusing you now?"

"Yes. You are."

He pulled out his phone and it showed me staring dead at his dick. I was mortified.

"Am I still accusing you? Or are you just guilty?"

I held my head down and tried to look as if I was busy reading my tablet.

"Yeah, that's what I thought. Busted."

He chuckled and I wanted to scream.

"Okay, you got me. One up for you."

"I'm always going to be a step ahead."

This Thug Love Got Me Trippin: A Belize Christmas

"It doesn't matter because you're not my real boyfriend. If we were together, I'm afraid we'd kill each other."

"I feel the same way." He was quiet for a moment and then he spoke again. "Tell me about this dude you're trying to win back. What's his name?"

"Knox. And he's my ex fiancé."

"Okay and why do you want him back?"

"You're nosey."

"Shit, I'm just trying to help. I skimmed your thesis and I didn't see anything about him or your relationship with him."

"Because I don't like talking about him."

"Then, how the hell do you plan on getting him back?"

"What do you care? You're leaving as soon as we land in Belize." I had folded my arms and poked out my lip before I knew it.

"Stop being a big ass baby. I was just playing with you. I'm a man of my word. My word is bond. Now, get out of your damn feelings and tell me about this nicca that you're trying to make jealous. What's your plan?"

I giggled. "I don't have one."

Ace eyed me strangely before he cracked up. "So, let me get this straight. You hired me to make your ex jealous and you haven't even thought about how you would get him back." He laughed even harder. "And I'm the stupid one, right?"

I cut my eyes in his direction. "I'll come up with something or I'll wing it just like you're doing."

"Whatever, girl, you'll never be like me. You're a planner. Winging it ain't your thang so get that thought out of your head."

The airplane finally landed in Belize. Ace grabbed his carry-on and walked off the plane. I cut my eyes at his rude ass because he didn't even attempt to be a gentleman and get my carry-on for me. He was already at baggage claim when I arrived.

"You could have gotten my carry-on," I sneered.

"You're right. I could have, but I didn't."

Just then, my bag was coming around the carousel. "Well, you can make it up to me now by getting my bag for me."

This Thug Love Got Me Trippin: A Belize Christmas

"Make what up to you? You're not handicapped. You shouldn't have packed all that shit if you couldn't handle it."

"Never mind, I'll get it myself."

By the time I went to grab my large suitcase, I missed the handle and it kept on going, nearly ripping my fingers off.

"Shit!" I hollered.

Ace fell out laughing. He thought it was so damn funny that I tripped over my own two feet, missed getting the bag, and tumbled onto the carousel before I landed on my ass for the second time today. I was so defeated that I didn't even attempt to get my bag this time when it came around. Ace reached out and yanked my bag off as if it was no big deal.

"C'mon, let's go. I'm ready to enjoy Belize."

We made our way to our tour guide who was standing next to my brother. He must've just got here too. He couldn't have been on our flight unless he was in coach.

"Eli!" I screamed.

"Sassy!" he yelled back. "Hey sis. Long time no see"

"Sassy?" Ace retorted. "Yeah, that name definitely fits you."

Eli hugged me tight. "You looking good, sis. Who is the dude behind you?"

I was all smiles until Eli asked me who Ace was. For a minute, I had forgotten all about him. "Oh, this is my boyfriend, Ace. And Ace, this is my brother Eli."

"That's right. I'm Sassy's boyfriend," Ace said with a smirk. I hated he found out about my nickname.

Eli side-eyed me. Then, he dapped up Ace and glared at him. "I think I know you from somewhere. Are you from Chicago too?"

"Yep. Born and raised."

Eli smiled, taking a liking to Ace already. He hated Knox so it would figure. "Cool. You play ball?"

"Of course, what young black man doesn't?" Ace chuckled and so did Eli.

"Aight. We gotta get a game when we get back home."

"You got it."

This Thug Love Got Me Trippin: A Belize Christmas

The tour guide drove us as far as we could go and then we transferred to a boat which took us to our private island: Royal Belize.

"Damn, y'all got money like for real, for real. Look at this shit. It's fuckin' amazing."

Eli grinned. "Welcome to Belize, bruh. I assume this is your first time. You're going to love it."

Ace grinned too. "This shit is unreal, bro. I ain't never been nowhere like this before."

"Well, I'll catch you guys later. I need to change and meet my boo at airport. She caught a later flight."

Eli started walking towards the Little House but quickly turned around, looking at me.

"Aye Sas. I'm glad you brought someone because Knox brought someone too. His fiancée."

My heart dropped to the pit of my stomach and I wanted to cry when Eli said that. I had no idea that Knox had moved on. No one had mentioned that part to me. What was I going to do now? This whole time I was coming back here to win him back. How was I going to do that when he had a whole fiancée here with him?

"You okay?" Ace asked, quickly noticing my change in mood.

"Yeah," I lied. "I guess I'll have to fight harder to win him back."

Chapter 9

Cassie "Sassy" Treyton

"I'm hungry," I said, ready to sink my teeth into a fat juicy burger. I was always watching my figure but, now that I was on vacation, I was going to eat good and stuff my face with calories.

"Me too. I ain't ate shit since last night. A nicca's stomach is touching his back."

"Good. Let's go eat then."

Ace looked around as if he was trying to figure out where we were going to eat. "How does that work? Because from what I can see, we're on a small ass island surrounded by water. Are we going to catch our food and cook it? If so, I'm not down for that. I could have kept myself in Chicago."

Princess Diamond

I giggled like crazy. "No silly. You're so dramatic. We are going to catch the boat back to the mainland and eat. That's why the tour guide is waiting for us. She's our personal tour escort during our stay and we have other staff that wait on us as well."

The look on Ace's face was priceless.

"All that shit you were talking about me being bougie. Well, Mr. Hood, welcome to the finer things in life."

"Shit, I'm not even gone pretend like I know what this life is like. I'll put my damn pride to the side because I'm intrigued." A wide grin plastered across his face. "Show me more."

"Oh, I thought you were all thugged out," I reiterated in my best thug voice.

"Shorty, chill. We in Belize. My money is all in my pocket because this trip is on you. I'm just here to be your boyfriend."

"Fake boyfriend," I emphasized.

"Whatever the fuck. If you footing the bill on all this shit, I'm game. I know I was tripping before, but I wouldn't dare go home and miss out on all of this for nothing in the world. This place is amazing and I'm down to be whatever or whoever you want me to be and how long you want me to be it. As long as I get to enjoy this amazing trip, I really don't care. Yolo. Fuck it."

"Yolo," I repeated. "So, that means you're finally on board to be my fake boyfriend and not give me any shit about it?"

"I'm down. We're a team and we about to get your boo back. You just say the word. I got you."

"Does that mean you're going to stop fighting me too?"

Ace nodded. "Yep. You paid me to do a job and I'm going to do it." He bowed and I laughed. "Ace Hood at your service, your highness."

Ace held out his hand as a gesture of good faith and I put my hand into his, shaking it.

"I just have one request. Can we change clothes before we leave? I'm sweating my balls off."

I scrunched up my face and laughed. "Eww. We wouldn't want that."

He laughed too. "So, you been here before?"

"Yeah, once. Eli comes to Belize all the time."

"So, tell me about it?"

"Cool. All these are air-conditioned villas. It's all inclusive, which means it's already paid for. There is no extra charges for anything."

"What does anything mean?" I asked as we walked toward our villa.

"No extra charges for meals, snacks, or alcoholic or nonalcoholic beverages. Our concierge will take care of everything. We have an island manager, private chef, concierge, housekeeping, and a boat captain."

Ace screamed out in joy. "You're lying?"

"No, boyfriend, I'm not. And we have cell phones located in each villa with wireless Internet access that can be used at any time."

"This muthafucka is like heaven. Shit, I don't even want to go back home."

I giggled. "I'll admit. I had the same reaction when I first came here. It's like a dream come true."

We walked to our living quarters, which was the Big House. I had been to Belize before but never to this private island. It was gorgeous. Our villa had three separate bedrooms with private entrances and connecting doors. Each room had a king bed with air conditioning, a private

This Thug Love Got Me Trippin: A Belize Christmas

bathroom, patios, and a mini fridge. Not to mention, the ocean that surrounded the island. I showed him around the villa. He picked his room and I picked mine.

"After you change into something more comfortable, meet me by the boat in fifteen minutes."

Ace nodded and disappeared into his room with a wide grin. Exactly fifteen minutes later, I was walking towards the boat with my booty shorts on and a crop top. My long hair was pulled up into a twist on top of my head and I had sandals on that showed off my toes.

"You look beautiful," Ace said with a smirk.

"You're not so bad yourself. I see you wearing Nike from head to toe. I like your slides. I didn't expect you to have nice feet. Most men don't."

"I'm not most men, shorty," Ace said, helping me into the boat while the concierge took our bags to our room. I sat down on the boat next to Ace and he put his arm around me. Our tour guide took off full speed ahead.

"You're not so bad, Cassie. I mean, Sassy."

I laughed. "Same to you, Ace. I apologize

for calling you a thug."

"Well, you might be right about me being a thug. I was raised in the streets, so I am thuggish. However, I'm trying to change that image, change my ways, you know. Everyone from the hood don't want to stay hood like, feel me?"

"I feel that and I respect it too."

"So, where are your parents?"

"Oh, they're at the toy drive. We give gifts to children every Christmas. Usually, I come the day before so that I can participate, but that didn't happen this year. I just sent my gifts ahead of time. Anyway, you'll meet them later."

We smiled at each other and enjoyed a light conversation about nothing in particular while crossing the sea to Midtown Family Restaurant. I was starving when we walked in. Apparently, Ace was too. We were seated right away and ready to order.

"Sassy?" a familiar voice asked.

I turned my head and saw one of my childhood friends from back home.

"Oh, my goodness. Lima. Girl, it's so good to see you. You waitress here?"

"Yes. I married a handsome Belizean man."

This Thug Love Got Me Trippin: A Belize Christmas

Lima held up her small wedding ring and smiled. "I got two kids and I've never been happier."

A twinge of jealousy ran through me. Here we were the same age and she was married with two kids and never been happier. Yet, I was a career oriented lawyer with no family to call my own. I held back my tears as she showed me pictures of her kids and her man.

"I'm happy for you, Lima," I lied and buried my face in the menu.

Ace scanned the menu and ordered first. "Hey Lima, let me get a Jumbo Boneless Pork Loin with everything. Make sure it has cheese too. Oh, and I also want a turtle cheesecake."

"And for you, Sassy," Lima asked.

"I want a Jumbo Cheeseburger with the works." I stuck my tongue out playfully and Ace chuckled. "Fries with it. That'll be all."

"Thank you," the waitress said, taking our orders.

Ace stopped Lima by gently grabbing her arm. "Oh Lima, can you bring us a pitcher of whatever they have here that's strong and fruity?"

Lima winked at us. "Oh, you want the Panty Rippa."

I nearly choked on my spit. "The what? I'm not sure I want that. It sounds like I'd get pregnant drinking it." Just the thought of making out with Ace's fine ass had me ready to break out into a sweat.

"Is it that good?" Ace asked Lima, totally intrigued.

"The locals love it. I've had it numerous times. It's pretty good. I'd definitely recommend it, especially since you two are on vacation and you don't have to drive anywhere. I'll even make it extra strong."

"Sign me the fuck up then."

"You got it." Lima took the menus from us and smiled.

"You seem really excited about that drink," I said to Ace.

"And who knew you could eat like that?" Ace countered. "I thought all Sassy ate was salads and protein shakes. I had no idea you could eat your little butt off."

"Big butt," I added. "Don't play, I got an onion boo." I laughed. Anyone with two eyes could see that I didn't have the biggest butt, but was fat enough.

This Thug Love Got Me Trippin: A Belize Christmas

Ace bit his bottom lip, glaring at my backside. "You sure do. Looks soft too."

I reached over the table and smacked his arm. "Stop looking at my butt, fake boyfriend."

He smirked. "I can't help it. Your ass is nice. I'll admit, I thought about squeezing it a few times."

He winked and I shook my head.

"You're so nasty."

"You have no idea. I gets busy, baby. I'm like Trey, I invented sex."

I sucked my teeth. "Okay, you're doing the most now."

We both laughed and continue to joke around. We were so engrossed in our conversation that we didn't even see Lima come back with our food. It was so good that we ate in silence, stuffing our faces. I watched Ace as he ate, and I could sense that he wasn't feeling this plan with me and Knox. I'd bet any amount of money that he wondered why I was fighting for a man who was engaged.

"I bet you think I'm stupid for wanting a dude with a fiancée."

Ace shrugged. "It ain't my place to judge.

You love who you love." He looked as if he was going to keep silent, but he spoke again. "If Knox is such a great guy, why did you all break up anyway?"

I sighed and fought back tears. "He dumped me. He wanted me to be a stay at home wife and mother instead of practicing law."

"Okay, he's one of those types." Ace cut his eye to the ceiling. "What makes you think you can get this dickhead back?"

"I was thinking about quitting law and settling down with him, giving things a try his way."

Ace shook his head in disbelief. "I'm not a fan of you practicing law either. Clearly, you're not the best…"

I stabbed my fork at my plate to let him know that I didn't think what he said was funny, and he chuckled.

"Listen, I know first-hand how you represent your clients, so please don't go there. Anyway, with that being said, I don't think you should give up your career for some arrogant nicca."

"I never said he was arrogant."

This Thug Love Got Me Trippin: A Belize Christmas

"You didn't have to. Any man who would make you choose him or your career is definitely full of himself."

"Yeah well, I want to be a mother and wife too someday. Knox is the guy to give me that."

Ace stared at me funny. "If you say so. I think you're making a big mistake but, then again, what do I know? I'm just a thug."

Our eyes met and, for a second, I thought I saw a hit of envy. It couldn't be, I convinced myself. Ace was only here because I paid him. I stared at Ace with sad eyes. I wasn't sure why I cared what he thought.

"The heart wants what the heart wants," he conceded.

I was about to comment when I looked up and saw Knox. He was right here in the restaurant, walking towards us.

"Don't turn around but here comes Knox."

Ace stiffened in his seat. He looked like he wanted to turn around, but he stopped himself. "Damn, is he stalking you? I don't like this shit."

Ace's face frowned up and I got the impression once again that he might be jealous. I couldn't deal with Ace or his fake feelings right now. I needed to pay attention to the man I came here to win back. I hadn't seen Knox since last Christmas and he looked damn good in his khakis, tucked in polo shirt, and sandals.

"Sassy!" he exclaimed, walking up to our table. "I know that beautiful face anywhere."

Immediately, I gushed, stood, and hugged him. "It's so nice to see you."

He smiled, checking me out. His eyes lingered on my breasts and ass a little too long. "Likewise. I wondered how things would be when we finally saw each other again. I hope it doesn't feel too awkward."

"No, silly," I lied. "Of course not. We're still friends, right?"

"Sure are."

Being in Knox's presence had me blushing. It seemed as if he'd changed a lot since I'd last seen him.

"I miss you," Knox admitted.

"I miss you too," I admitted as well. "When you dumped me, you acted like you didn't care."

"I always cared and I will never stop. I'm glad you came."

"Me too."

This Thug Love Got Me Trippin: A Belize Christmas

"I wanted to talk to you. I got some things I want to say."

"Wow!" I beamed. "That's exactly how I've been feeling too. You know I was thinking…"

Ace cleared his throat, interrupting my flow. I was just about to get my man back when my fake boyfriend cock blocked. What was he doing? And what kind of hating ass shit was this?

Chapter 10

Ace Hood

Sassy was all into Knox until I cleared my throat, breaking her fixation on his lame ass. Sassy stood there stuck on stupid as I smirked at her. She had to be crazy if she thought I was going to sit back and be disrespected. Fake boyfriend or not, Knox was disrespectful as fuck. He saw us sitting here eating. He didn't even bother to acknowledge me.

Something wasn't right about this guy. I had a feeling Sassy was wasting her time. She could do much better. I truly didn't see what she saw in him. He was a rich nerd with no swag and he talked white as fuck. Knox glared at me and I narrowed my eyes at him. I didn't want to, but I did what her boyfriend would do. I stuck out my hand and introduced myself to him.

"Hi, I'm Ace. Sassy's boyfriend. And you are?"

Knox's light skin turned pale as he looked from Sassy to me in shock. His hand lightly gripped mine. "Oh, okay. It's nice to meet you man. I didn't know Sassy was dating someone. The last I heard, she was single."

Knox was staring Sassy down and she just stood there looking mortified and uneasy, so I took complete control, slipping my arm around Sassy's neck.

"Yeah, bro. I couldn't turn down the chance to meet Sassy's family and spend Christmas together. And by the way, who are you again?"

Knox wore a simple look on his face as I continued.

"Oh, wait a minute. You're her ex-boyfriend right?"

"Ex-fiancé," Knox mumbled.

He had no idea that I was petty as hell and king of clap backs. "That's right. I heard Eli mentioning you. I remember now. You're Knox. Where is your fiancée? Isn't she here?" I asked and pretended to look around for her. "I'd like to meet her. In fact, maybe you two could join us at our table?"

My little speech seemed to snap Sassy out of her love-induced trance with Knox. Hearing that he had a fiancée seemed to snap her back to reality.

"Yeah, where is your fiancée, Knox?" Sassy asked with her arms folded in anger.

Knox gulped down the lump in his throat. "Um, she caught a late flight, so she won't be here until after Christmas Eve dinner."

"Isn't that convenient?" I asked, stirring up the suspicion.

Sassy and I stared Knox down until he began to feel very uncomfortable. "Um, I better go. I'll see you tonight at dinner."

"Okay, bro. Sounds like a plan. Who knows, maybe you're fiancée will surprise you for dinner. That'll be nice."

Knox scurried away and Sassy paid the tab. She was upset with me, but I didn't care. I was upset with her too. I remained silent until we got back on the boat. Then, I decided to speak my peace.

"You know if I was your real boyfriend, I

would be ready to snatch your fake eyelashes off."

"And if you were my real boyfriend, I wouldn't be paying you to make Knox jealous. I can't believe you interrupted us. What were you thinking?"

"I was thinking that you looked like a fool. If I'm your boyfriend, then I needed to act like I was one. No man I know was going to sit there and watch his woman get all googly eyes with the next nicca and he just sits there like a bump on a log. Look at me."

Sassy stared in my direction with angry eyes.

"Do I look like the type of person who would let the next man hit on my girl in front of me? Hell no. If this were for real, I would have kicked Knox's nerdy looking ass."

"Well, you do what I paid you to do and nothing more. That's why I gave you instructions on what to do."

"I'm not a puppet. I already told you that. You take my help the way I'm going to give it to you or leave it."

"I'll leave it then."

"Fine!"

"Fine!"

I didn't want to show her that I was upset and a slightly bit jealous. The way she looked at Knox was special. That's something I'd always wanted from a woman. I thought I had that with my ex-fiancée, so I understood why Sassy was jumping through hoops for Knox. I just didn't feel like he deserved her but, then again, dudes like him always got women because they had money. Cash rules the world. That's why I was working so hard to get my bread up. The only money that I had was from Sassy. Thinking about the fact that Knox could give her the world and I had to lean on her paying for everything made me feel some type of way. I promised myself when my app got off the ground, I was going to pay her back every cent she ever spent. My pride wouldn't let me keep the money free and clear. I was looking at the ten thousand dollars as a loan.

The boat docked at Royal Belize and Sassy jumped out before I could, and ran to her bedroom entrance. I didn't even bother to chase after her. She was throwing another tantrum, playing the victim once again. If anyone should be upset, it should be me. I was feeling the rum. I couldn't run if I wanted to. The sun was beaming and a nicca needed a serious nap. I made my way into my bedroom entrance and threw myself across my bed.

From what I could tell, this was going to be the longest two days of my life. I was starting to wonder if the money was even worth the trouble. Belize was gorgeous, but I wasn't about to enjoy it because I was stuck with a spoiled brat, her weak ass ex-boyfriend, and pretending to be some shit that I wasn't. That whole combination didn't made a damn bit of sense and it was a recipe for disaster.

I was going to kick Cakes' ass when I returned. I would call him and cuss his ass out, but my damn phone wasn't getting any reception all the way out here in the middle of nowhere. When we went back to the mainland, it just roamed. The only time I seemed to get service was at the airport.

Chapter 11

Cassie "Sassy" Treyton

If I hadn't paid Ace's ass to be here, I would have kicked him off the island. I wasn't that stupid though. Since I paid for his ass, he was going to stay, hear my mouth, and deal with all the drama that I might have going on. Telling him to leave would be too easy.

Besides, a part of me liked the fact that Ace stood up to Knox and claimed me. I was sure it made Knox think. I could have had any man I wanted, just like Knox knew he could have any woman he wanted. I might not have liked the way Ace responded to my conversation with Knox, but he definitely got Knox's attention. I saw the fury in his eyes. Hopefully, it would make him go harder and fight for me like a real man should. Dump his fiancée and claim me as his bride to be once again.

I didn't mean to talk to Ace like that. I was sure I hurt his feelings. I lashed out at him because I was thinking about the fact that Knox moved on so quickly. He found another fiancée, which had me thinking twice about why we really broke up. Was this bitch in the picture all along? Or did he really move on that fast? All of this shit was making my head spin. Meditating always cleared my mind so that's what I did. Once I meditated for about forty-five minutes, I read my law journal until I drifted off to sleep.

By the time I woke up, it was Christmas Eve dinner. I sure hoped that Eli told Ace what was going on because I wasn't telling him shit. He could stay in his room and starve for all I cared. Yeah, that was petty, but so what? I was used to getting my way and I felt like if he had followed my thesis as he called it, things would have went a lot smoother.

Holiday tunes played as I made my way to the Christmas Eve dinner. Eli and Ace were already drinking and talking a short distance away from my parents. An envious twinge raced through me because I felt like someone should have woke me up so that I could have been here when Ace first met them.

"Hi honey," my mother said, standing to hug me. "I really like Ace," she whispered. "He's a good choice and very handsome too. You two will make some pretty babies."

"Mom!" I shrieked.

She smiled and sat back down next to my father.

"There's my baby girl," my daddy said, patting his lap.

I sat down and wrapped my arm around my daddy like I always did.

"How are you, daddy?"

"I'm good, baby girl. I'm even better now that I see you. He kissed me on the cheek and whispered in my ear, "I've been giving that Ace fella the blues, but he seems good for you. I like him a lot. You made a good choice baby girl."

I looked over at Ace and he smiled, raising his drink in my direction. He was standing there talking to Eli and some bimbo looking hoe that I assumed was his girlfriend.

This Thug Love Got Me Trippin: A Belize Christmas

"Who is that?" I asked my mother, nodding my head towards Eli's girlfriend.

"Girl, please don't get me started. That's your brother's stripper girlfriend."

"What?" I exclaimed. "Are you serious?"

My mother gulped down her wine. "I wish I was lying, honey. I don't know where I went wrong with that boy. He refuses to do anything right."

"Leave him alone, Clara," my father defended. "He's twenty-four and having fun. Surely, he's not going to marry a tramp like that. She's all body and no brains."

"What?" I asked for a second time. "She's stupid too?"

"Shhhhh," my mother hushed. "I don't want no problems with that ghetto bunny."

I fell out laughing, tickled pink because of what my mother said. Eli's girlfriend looked hella ghetto. She had on a tie-up dress that was so tight that I could see her nipples poking through and the outline of her ass injections.

"It's time to eat everyone," the chef said.

Right on time, Knox and his parents wandered in. They greeted everyone and I noticed the nasty nonverbal exchange between Ace and Knox. Then, Eli whispered something in Ace's ear and they laughed like best buddies. Everyone made their way to the eating area and we were seated. All of the parents sat by each other. I sat close to Ace and Eli. Knox sat opposite of me.

"Excuse me," I said to Eli's girlfriend. "My brother is so rude. I'm Sassy. What's your name?"

"Verde," she said with a ghetto flare.

I just smiled and stared at the food that was being presented before us. This trick was Eli's problem. She was pretty though.

"The spread look nice," Knox said about the food, but he was looking dead at me.

"It does look good," my father commented.

We had fruits, vegetables, meats, and sides. Anything you could ask for, we had on our table. I opted for shrimp, salmon, steak, salad, and mixed fruits. I was going to continue to drink water, but I needed something stronger because every time I looked up, my eyes met with Knox or Ace. It was evident that they were both fighting for my attention and, for some odd reason, I felt torn. Ace was growing on me quicker than I cared to admit. We had a chemistry that was flourishing. Then, there was Knox. My first love and the man I'd always wanted to marry.

Dessert was brought out and most of us were already stuffed. I ate a few bites and called it quits with the food. Of course, all of the men, including my brother, Knox, and Ace, were digging into the sweets. I would never understand how men could eat everything in sight and still remain skinny. If I stared at something with too many calories, it felt like it went straight to my hips just because I looked at it. That's why I constantly watched what I ate and worked out like crazy. I wasn't about to be one of those fat and out of shaped chicks that always complained about her weight.

"It's time for some Christmas fun. The ornament exchange is first," my mother said, clapping her hands like a child. She loved Christmas, so she was super festive. My mother motioned for Knox's mother to join her. My father and his father got up and followed after our mothers.

Princess Diamond

"What's an ornament exchange?" Ace asked. He was totally clueless.

I was about to explain when Eli cut me off. "Yo, it's the best. So, our parents pick out ornaments and put our names on them. Whoever you get, you have to say the engraved words on the back and three nice things about them. You have to give that person a hug and a kiss and place the ornament on the tree, wishing that person Christmas blessings."

Ace still looked confused. "Okay, sounds like fun."

"It is. I love seeing the looks on people's faces when they get someone they don't like or don't know. It's hilarious."

Ace forced a smile and glanced at me before taking another sip of his spiked egg nog.

Eli clearly knew that Ace was still confused because he continued to explain. "Think of it like an ornament fortune cookie. The ornaments are randomly made with the sayings and our names are etched on them. It's a family fun tradition. You'll like it."

Our parents came back with gift wrapped ornaments inside of two large present boxes.

Everyone picked one and, once we all had our ornaments, it was time to start.

"Each person has a number on their box. The person with one starts, then two, and so on," my mother stated.

"Oh, I'm going first!" Verde screamed, about to tear open her gift. She was jumping around too much. I just hoped her damn tits didn't fall out at the table. She had two hints of fabric holding her titties in place.

My mother quickly busted her bubble. "No honey. You're not first. Read the number on your box. The number on your box says five. That means you're the fifth person to go."

"Sorry about that, mom," Eli expressed, trying to save face. He knew his bimbo was about to catch a few words from mom.

"Bimbo," my mother mumbled. I didn't think Verde heard her, but I sure did and I wanted to laugh.

I looked down at my gold wrapped box and saw that it had a big fat number one. I didn't want to go first. I was already feeling uncomfortable with the stares from Ace and Knox all through dinner. Going first felt like a spotlight was placed on me and I was beginning to sweat.

"It looks like it's me," I voiced, slowly tearing off the gift wrap and pulling my ornament out of the wrapping. "I have…Rudolph?" I asked more than said. "Who is this?"

"Did I make a typo?" my mother inquired. "I could have sworn you said your boyfriend's name was Rudolph. I was surprised when I was introduced to Ace."

Damn, I couldn't believe I forgot the stupid name that I made up for my fake boyfriend.

"No, mom, it's my fault," I said, trying to save face. I giggled nervously and hoped that no one could see me sweating. "Sorry about that everyone. I was multi-tasking and accidently texted the wrong name. Please forgive me, Ace."

Ace seemed cool as a fan about the mix up while I was ready to jump out of my skin. Everyone seemed to overlook the name mix up except for Knox, who grimaced. Ace looked at me with those sexy bedroom eyes and grinned as I held his ornament in my hands. He looked flattered that I had picked him and I felt the butterflies return. I wasn't sure why I had those feelings because nothing was going on between us, or was it?

"C'mon, now sweetie," my father urged.

"Yes sir. Um, Ace, I want to say to you that all I want for Christmas is you. You're handsome, fun, and carefree." I stood up and walked around the table to him and hugged him. Electricity ran through my body as we embraced. It was very unusual and I couldn't deny the feelings that I was starting to develop for him.

"Merry Christmas and New Year Blessings."

Ace squeezed me even tighter before he let me go. I walked over to the Christmas tree and placed my ornament on it with a smile.

"Okay, who is next?" my mother asked.

Ace looked down at his box. "It looks like it's me."

He quickly unwrapped and held his ornament in the air.

"I have Sassy."

"Really?" Knox exclaimed.

Ace held it up again, showing my name. For some reason, my eyes darted to Knox who was stabbing his dessert plate with a fork. My eyes shifted back to Ace, who was about to read.

"Sassy. Christmas only comes once a year. The love that I have for you comes only once in a lifetime. You're beautiful, very smart, and any man would be lucky to have you. Live your dreams and don't settle for less."

Ace stood up and bumped Knox's chair hard as hell as he made his way over to me. "Sorry about that," he announced with a sly smirk as he stood in front of me. "Merry Christmas and New Year Blessings."

He leaned in as if he was going to hug me, but I was taken by surprise when his lips touched mine. There was a spark and I felt as if my legs were going to give out. Ace noticed that I was wobbly and helped me back into my seat before he hung his ornament on the tree.

The rest of the ornament exchange was a blur. All I could think about was Ace. I didn't know why he kissed me and I didn't know why I liked it so much. My parents seemed to approve. They really liked Ace. I could tell by their interactions with him.

This Thug Love Got Me Trippin: A Belize Christmas

While we were decorating the Christmas cookies, Knox asked if he could speak to me in private. I felt like this was a sign because silently, I had been praying for Knox to step up and claim me before Ace whisked me away. We walked outside away from the dining area so that we could talk in private.

"I'm glad you finally asked to speak to me alone," I admitted. "I wanted to talk to you earlier and clear some things up."

"First, I want to say you look amazing. When I came here to Belize, all I wanted to do was see you. Then, I met Ace."

That kind of rubbed me the wrong way. "Why did you say it like that?"

Knox smiled. "Well, I was hoping that you came this way to see me, and that we could spend some time together while we were here.."

"Really? Did you come this way to see me?"

"Of course."

"But, how could that be when you have a fiancée?"

"Well, that's what I wanted to talk to you about. Your feelings matter to me. I want to keep it real and tell you before the next person does."

"What's that?"

"I want to apologize for breaking off our engagement. I felt as if it were my fault. You loved me so much and-"

It was as if a revelation hit me as he was talking. "You cheated, didn't you?"

"I… I…"

My mouth fell open and I couldn't close it. I was really flabbergasted. "Was it with this heffa that you're engaged to now?" I asked, feeling my anger rise.

"Um, sorta."

I felt the hot tears ready to fall. "That means you cheated, Knox. I thought we had something real? We didn't because you cheated."

"It wasn't like that."

"Then, what was it like?"

Knox stood there looking dumb as hell while I fought back tears.

"Just answer this one question truthfully. Is the woman that you cheated on me with the same bitch that you're engaged to now?"

Knox held down his head and answered, "Yes."

This Thug Love Got Me Trippin: A Belize Christmas

"Go fuck yourself, Knox. I'm done with your ass."

I tried to storm away, but the sand had me looking slow and stupid with tears blinding my sight. My master plan to get my ex back had failed miserably and I felt broken. What was I going to do now?

.

Chapter 12

Ace Hood

Sassy was gone for at least an hour. I had no idea where she went. By the time dinner was over, I made my way back to our villa and saw her lying across the bed crying. One thing popped into my mind, that nicca Knox. I know he had something to do with her tears.

"The fuck did that punk ass nicca Knox do?"

I must've startled Sassy because she jumped up from the bed in shock.

"Ace, dammit, don't ever do that again."

She held her heart as if I'd almost given her a heart attack.

"My bad, I heard you crying and came to see what was up with you. You never came back to dinner."

This Thug Love Got Me Trippin: A Belize Christmas

Sassy flopped back down on the bed and I took a seat next to her.

"What happened?" I inquired. "Did that nicca put his hands on you?"

"No, nothing like that," she cried.

"Then, what was it?"

"I found out that he cheated on me while we were engaged. That's why he dumped me. He was in love with another woman."

"Are you serious right now?" This shit had me fired up.

Sassy nodded her head and that made me even more livid.

"What you want me to do? I'll kick the shit out of him, just say the word. I've been wanting to put my hands on him since I saw him."

"No, that's not necessary. It just hurts to find out the truth. I came here to win him back and I find out he has a fiancée, who he cheated on me with when we were engaged and that was the reason why he wanted to talk to me."

"Wait. Wait a minute." I had to hold down my head and let out a nervous laugh because this Knox dude was a real jerk. "He didn't even try to dump her and win you back?"

"Nope," Sassy cried. "It was like hc wanted to date us both."

"Fuck him. He is not the man for you. He never was and God did you a favor by getting rid of that loser. You were about to give up your whole career for this cornball."

Ace reached over and dabbed my face with some tissue. "Listen, I know that I was hard on you. I said some foul shit and-"

"No, Ace, I need to be apologizing to you. I judged you from the beginning and I was wrong. We got off to the wrong start, but you're a nice guy. I'm glad you came. Honestly."

"I feel the same way."

"Is that why you kissed me?" she asked with a twinkle in her eye.

"Maybe."

I snickered. She had me nervous. I ain't felt this nervous in such a long time. Sassy was staring at me with sincerity and I was receiving it. Things had definitely shifted for us. I reached for her hand and she slipped hers into mine.

"It seemed like the right thing to do," I said, honestly.

This Thug Love Got Me Trippin: A Belize Christmas

"Did you mean all those nice things that you said when you read the ornament?"

"Did you?"

We both fell out laughing. A fun, gut-releasing laugh that only two people who are connected would do. An inside type of joke laugh.

"Yes," I answered first, staring deep into her eyes. "I meant what I said, I enjoyed the kiss and-"

"And what?" Sassy said with some sass. Her cute little pouty lips and sexy smile.

"And what if I want another one?"

"I'll give you another kiss if you go swimming with me."

I raised my eyebrows because my dick was already hard and she wanted to see me in some trunks. I didn't know if that shit was going to be a good idea.

"Alright. I'm with it. Let's do it."

Sassy jumped up from the bed and cheered. I could tell she used to be a cheerleader back in high school. She was limber as hell and I could think of a thousand different ways to put her body to good use.

"Let me leave before all that jumping around gets you jumped."

I winked at her and she threw her pillow at me.

"Meet me outside in five minutes or I'm going to come looking for you. Don't stand me up and don't fall asleep. And I don't want to hear no lame excuses about why you can't go because you can't swim."

"Girl, who you talking to? I've already hit the beach. You're late. And for your info, I can swim. My mother loves to swim and she taught me how when I was in diapers."

"Okay," Sassy said. She was looking and feeling much better. That's all I really wanted.

I felt Sassy's eyes on me as I strutted out, so I turned around and caught her staring at me. That made me feel very confident. I winked at her and retreated to my bedroom. I wished I could call Cakes so bad. Shit had been so all over the place and I just wanted to share this experience with him. I had some real thinking to do. Sassy was wearing me down and I was doing the same with her.

This Thug Love Got Me Trippin: A Belize Christmas

I grabbed a bottle of champagne and hit the beach. Sassy was already out on the beach when I approached her from behind, grabbing her around her waist. She nuzzled back into me and we slowly walked into the water together. We were drinking from the bottle of champagne and splashing water everywhere. Laughing, joking, and having a ball.

At this moment, it felt like we were a couple. She was a totally different person than who I met initially. This was the real her and I was really digging it. The flirting was very heavy. She was lusting for me and I was lusting for her.

I tossed our second bottle of champagne into the sand and held Sassy close in my arms. "What are you thinking right now?"

She leaned in so close to me and our lips touched. We shared a passionate kiss for a few seconds.

"It's been a long time, Ace. I want you, but only if you really want me too."

My dick had been semi-hard most of the trip, but now it was bricked up. "I've wanted you from the moment you fell in the airport. I wanted to lay on top of you then and pipe you down."

"I need to feel you inside of me. Right now, that's the only thing that I'm missing. Only you can give me what I'm craving."

"Do you really mean that? What about Knox?"

"What about him? You're my boyfriend?" she giggled.

"He's not standing here with me right now, you are."

It was something about the way she said boyfriend that felt real. It had my heart thumping and my dick stiffening.

"Are you sure?" I asked her, not wanting to take advantage of her. "We can just go back to your room and I can hold you until you fall asleep. We don't have to go there, you know?"

Sassy looked at me with lust-filled eyes. "Ace. I want you. I've been wanting you."

"I want you too. But, is this really the right time?"

"Why wouldn't it be? We're on a beautiful island, surrounded by a beach and a gorgeous sea. This is the perfect place to make love. Are you scared?"

I smirked. "Daddy ain't never scared."

This Thug Love Got Me Trippin: A Belize Christmas

"Well, let me kickstart this party."

Sassy stood up and undid her bikini top and it fell to the floor, exposing her perky breasts. Next, she took over her bottoms and stood before me nude.

"Are you going to take off your trunks or do I have to take them off for you?"

I stood up boldly and let my trunks fall to the ground. Sassy's eyes landed on my dick and it was on. I walked up on her and kissed her like only I could. Hungrily, she kissed me back.

Things definitely heated up quickly because Sassy spread her legs, inviting my fingers to slip inside her wetness. She moaned and I slid inside of her deeper.

"Damn, you're wet. That pussy ready for me, huh?"

"Yes, Ace," she moaned. "Fuck me."

"Not yet, shorty. I need to taste this pussy first."

I pulled her over to the bed and pulled her on top of me, so she was straddling my face. I kissed her inner thighs as she tried to lower her pussy onto my tongue. Firmly, I held her in place so that I was in control. She balanced her goodies over my mouth as I teased her. I kissed everywhere but her clit because I knew that's what she wanted me to kiss. I was driving her wild because she was doing everything to sit them fat pussy lips on my face, but I wouldn't let her.

"Stop, playing, Ace and let me feel that tongue."

I smacked her ass and kissed her lower lips. "I'm not playing with you. I'm enjoying every inch of your body. There's no rush. We got all night."

"I'm horny, Ace. Please."

I pecked her lower lips again but still hadn't tongued her pearl like she wanted me to. Spreading her engorged lips, I slid one finger inside of her sweet spot and she shuddered.

"Feel good?"

"Yes," she said, grinding against my finger.

She was so wet that I had no choice but to slip another finger inside of her, just so I could keep up the pace. Sassy rolled her hips on my finger.

"Put your lips on it."

This Thug Love Got Me Trippin: A Belize Christmas

"On what?" I questioned. I knew what she wanted, but I wanted to tease her even more. "Tell me what you want, shorty. Tell me what you want me to do."

"Suck on my pussy."

I began licking her fat pussy lips. "Like that?"

"No," she protested. "Spread my lips."

I opened up her puffy lips. "Now what?"

"Flick your tongue across my pearl."

I stuck out my tongue and ran it across her pearl. "Like that?"

"Ssssshhhh. Yes, just like that."

I wrapped my arms around her hips and locked her pussy in place so that I could suck on it the way I wanted to. I licked, sucked, slurped, fingered, and tongued her pussy until she busted on my face.

"Oh. Oh. Oh. Oh. Mmmmmmyyyyyy, ACE! I'm cumming!"

Sassy bucked her slick pussy across my tongue and beard as she coated my face with juices. I flipped her pretty ass over and pinned her down, eating her pussy from the back. She tried to run away because her clit was still sensitive. It didn't take long before she was throwing her pussy back on my tongue and I was catching her cum.

Once I was satisfied that she was wet enough, I slid into her tight pussy. When I say that she was tight, I meant she was virgin tight. I wanted to ask her when was the last time that she had sex, but she was moaning so wildly that I didn't want to disrupt the mood with something stupid so I let it go and concentrated on anything other than her tight, gushy pussy.

No woman had ever felt the way Sassy did. Being inside of her was indescribable. It was as if we were having sex on a cloud or something. At first, I thought I was tripping, but Sassy confirmed what I was feeling when she started yelling out all these crazy things like: *I love you Ace. Your dick is the best. I'm in heaven.* I was sure that she was dickmatized, but it still felt good to hear her moan the shit while I was deep inside of her. I palmed her ass and pounded her pussy, as if I was the only one who knew my way to her sweet spot.

"Oh shit!" Sassy hollered. "I'm about to cum again, Ace."

This Thug Love Got Me Trippin: A Belize Christmas

I kept stroking her at the same pace and the same depth until her body convulsed and she fell face first on the bed out of breath. I was about to cum too, so I kept on pounding her until I couldn't hold back any longer. I pulled out and shot my babies on her soft ass. I collapsed on top of her and we curled up, sticky and satisfied, falling fast asleep after our sexual bliss.

Chapter 13

Cassie "Sassy" Treyton

I woke up and my stomach hurt like hell.

"How much did I drink?"

I held my head and felt like crap. I couldn't believe how messed up I was. I didn't remember much. I sat on the bed with my head pounding, thinking about what happened the night before. I remember crying and Ace came in to comfort me. He asked me to join him at the beach. I put on my bikini and he had on his trunks. We were flirting and kissing and…"

I gasped.

"Did I… did I have sex with him?"

I gasped again. I remembered bits and pieces of us getting buck wild last night.

This Thug Love Got Me Trippin: A Belize Christmas

I was so embarrassed. This was the reason why I didn't drink champagne. I never remembered shit afterwards. Wine was my friend. Champagne was my enemy. I picked my head up off the pillow and groaned. I couldn't face my parents like this. Not on Christmas morning.

Knock. Knock. Knock.

"Who is it?" I yelled and then held my head from the pain.

"Sis!" Eli screamed, making my head pound even more. "Mom and dad are waiting on you to serve breakfast."

"Don't come in, Eli. I'm not decent."

"I wouldn't dare. I don't want to throw up."

I wanted to laugh, but I couldn't. My hangover wouldn't allow me to.

"You sound like you had a wild night with Ace, sis."

"Ugh!" I groaned. "Leave me alone, Eli."

He laughed and tapped the wall like we did when we were kids to let me know he was leaving. Once my brother left, I drug myself out of bed and scrambled to the shower. Literally, I felt like shit and I needed to sober up immediately before my parents noticed.

Princess Diamond

After a long cold shower and two cups of coffee, I was ready to join my family for breakfast. I wasn't one-hundred percent, but I wasn't able to fake until I could make it.

"It took you long enough," my mother said with a frown. "We almost started eating without you."

"Sorry mom. I was up late last night."

"What were you doing up so late?" she countered.

I didn't expect her to ask what I was doing, so I was stumped. My eyes met with Ace and all I could think about was what we did last night, and why wasn't he as tore back as I was?

"Mrs. Treyton, we went swimming and that knocked Sassy out. Belize is very relaxing. I didn't wake her because I felt like she needed her rest. She'd been complaining about being so tired lately, working late and stuff."

My mother looked from Ace to me and smiled. "That's right, honey. I forgot all about your late hours. You probably did need the rest." My mother stood up and patted my hand lovingly. "Thank you, Ace. I must admit, you've been a pleasant surprise on this trip. I see why my baby is so crazy about you. She can't keep her eyes off you and you can't keep your eyes off her. I hope there is wedding bells in the near future and plenty of pretty grandbabies."

"Mom!"

"Chile, please. I'm going to speak my mind."

Ace snickered, but I was mortified. Eli chuckled as well and Verde was staring at her nails. She was just as clueless as ever. I was so glad that the breakfast only included our family. Knox and his parents weren't coming by until later on for Christmas dinner.

I didn't think I would be able to eat a thing when the spread was brought out. Pancakes, eggs, sausage, bacon, milk, orange juice, and coffee. Once I took one bite of my pancake, I went in. I mean, I ate enough for two people, stuffing myself. Surprisingly, I felt a lot better so maybe I just needed to eat and soak up all the liquor from the night before.

"Okay, everyone, it's time to exchange gifts."

We all shuffled from the table over to the Christmas tree with all the presents underneath. I began to panic because I realized that Ace didn't have a present for me. I had one for him, but I forgot to buy one for him so that he could give to me. Now, my stomach was upset again, but not because I was hungover. This time, it was anxiety and I felt a need to shit badly.

"I'll be right back?" I said, jumping up from the floor and running to the bathroom.

I made it just in time before I shit on myself. I think it was the coffee mixed with the pancakes. Or maybe it was the fact that I was just a pig after not eating enough because I got too drunk last night.

Bang! Bang! Bang! Bang!

"Leave me alone!" I hollered.

"Open up!" Ace said.

Was he for real? "Are you crazy? No! I'll be out in a minute."

"I said open up the damn door. Don't make me get loud. You know I can get ignorant. You better let me in or shit about to go left."

"Ugh! I hate you!"

"No, you don't. Open up."

I wiped myself as best as I could and jumped off the toilet. I needed to shit some more,

132

but this crazy dude was on the other side of the door about to cut a fool.

"Gotdamn!" Ace said with one arm over his nose and the other arm spraying like crazy.

"I don't want to hear shit about how it smells in here cuz you weren't invited. What do you want anyway?

"You straight?"

I flopped back down on the toilet and he rested against the sink with his shirt over his nose.

"What do you think? I'm on the toilet shitting my damn life away. Hell no, I'm not okay."

"You don't smell like you're okay either." He snickered and I wanted to take my shoe off and hit him in his damn head.

"Why are you here?"

"Your parents were worried about you. They said you didn't look too good, so I told them I would come and check on you. I wished I hadn't cuz you smell foul as fuck, shorty."

"Get out then and let me finish."

"Your shit smells so bad, you about to sink the damn island."

"Teeee. Heeee. You're so damn funny. Get out."

"You need me to get some Febreze or something. The last thing you want to do is come back and smell like boo boo. That's not to be confused with a term of endearment."

I sighed. "You came in here just to torture me, didn't you?"

"I mean, I was concerned until I smelled you. What the hell did you eat? You couldn't have eaten the same breakfast that we all ate. It's not even possible."

I took the toilet paper off the roll and threw it at him. "Get out."

Ace dodged the toilet paper with a laugh. "I'ma go so you can finish taking a dump."

"Get out!" I screamed with laughter. He had annoyed me so bad that I was actually laughing so hard that I was crying.

After I did my business, I returned to my family. Everyone was sitting around with presents in a pile before them. I sat down next to Ace and my pile of presents.

This Thug Love Got Me Trippin: A Belize Christmas

"I hoped you washed your hands?" Ace whispered. "Otherwise, you're going to have shit crumbs on your presents."

I smacked his arm and cracked up. He did too. When I looked up from laughing, my parents were smiling at me with approving looks.

"What's the joke?" Eli asked. "I want to laugh too."

"It's an inside joke," I replied.

We all opened our gifts and, as usual, I got a gift card from my brother and hefty checks from my parents. The last gift was from Ace. I didn't expect him to have anything for me, but he did.

"I want to tell you all that I didn't bring gifts with me because I thought I would be able to buy better gifts on the island. So, I went to an authentic Belize jewelry shop and had the owner make jewelry items based on each one of your personalities. She said it would bring good health and future blessings.

"Wow," my mother said, looking down at her necklace and earrings. "Thanks, Ace. It's perfect."

My father and brother seemed to like their warrior wristlets.

And my gift was awesome too. I could tell that Ace had spent more on my gift because of the rare shells and stones that were in it.

"Do you like it?" he asked me sincerely.

"Yes, I do. One of the best gifts I've ever gotten. I can tell you put a lot of thought into it."

"Thanks, bro," Eli exclaimed with a playful hit to Ace's shoulder.

"Why don't you show Ace around on our private boat? I'm sure he'd love to experience more to Belize than just this island. Take him on the jet skis too."

I smiled and stood to my feet. "Okay. That'll be fun."

"Don't worry about you're presents," my father stated. "They'll be in your rooms waiting for you. And don't be gone too long. Dinner starts in a few hours."

"Sure thing, daddy," I hugged my daddy and grabbed Ace's hand, leading the way.

*****

After Ace and I sailed the seas and road around the water on the jets, we were exhausted.

136

This Thug Love Got Me Trippin: A Belize Christmas

Both of us came back and took a nap. By the time we woke up, it was time to get dolled up for dinner. Christmas dinner was always fancy and formal.

Everyone was there, including Knox and his fiancée. He introduced me to her and I just knew that I would feel some type of way. Surprisingly, I didn't even care about her or him. My bond with Ace had grown so strong that I was more interested in him and what he was doing. Knox was no longer my concern anymore. His new fiancée could deal with his drama. I had washed my hands of his cheating ass, and it felt damn good to finally be free.

My father stood, getting everyone's attention. "I just want to say one last thing. This is our final day in Belize and our annual Christmas dinner," my father exclaimed with joy. "I'm glad that each and every one of you are here. During this time of year, it is important to be thankful and to be a blessing to others the way God would have wanted it to be. We do this in remembrance of Jesus Christ."

"To Jesus Christ," we all cheered.

"Continue to eat, have fun, and be merry. There is plenty of food, drinks, and desserts to go around," my father continued.

My mother cranked up the Christmas carols and everyone began singing. After a while, Eli tugged on Ace's arm, pulling him off to show him something as if he was his boyfriend instead of mine.

I was just about to make small talk with Verde when Knox approached me.

"Can I talk to you in private?"

"No," I exclaimed and started making my way to Verde. She was dumb as a box of rocks, but her conversation was better than talking to Knox. I was so turned off by his presence. I was upset at myself for even wanting this asshole back.

"Please," he begged.

I sighed. "Okay, but you have five minutes. Nothing more."

"Cool, that's all I need."

We stepped outside but, this time, I didn't walk far away. Last time, I nearly walked to the other side of the island so that we could talk. I hadn't planned on talking to him that long, so there was no need for us to walk that far away.

"What do you want?" I asked with my arms folded across my chest. I meant business and I wanted him to see it.

"You look beautiful," Knox said charmingly.

"What do you want?"

"Why are you so hostile? I just gave you a compliment."

"I don't want your compliment, Knox. I don't even want to talk to you. What do you want?"

"You seem really happy with Ace? Are you sure he's what you want?"

"Is that trick you cheated on me with who you want?"

Knox stared at me as if I still belonged to him. "So, you don't miss me? You don't miss what we had? The hot love making and the shopping trips? You could still have all that you know. I make enough money to give you the life that you deserve and those grandbabies that your mother keeps begging you for."

I exhaled so loud, steam should have come out of my nose. "No, not anymore. I don't want to be your side bitch. Or you play with my feelings until you decide to marry me."

"What changed between yesterday and today? Yesterday, you were feeling me. Today, it's like you can't stand the ground that I walk on. You know, something's different about you?"

Knox looked me over while I gave him the stank face.

"It's like… like… oh, hell nah. You fucked him, didn't you?"

"What do you mean?" I asked, caught off guard by his revelation. Was it that obvious that I had spread my legs to Ace? If he noticed, did my parents notice too?

"That's none of your business, Knox. What I do with my body is my business."

"You don't even have to answer me because I know that glow. Only dick can make you glow like that."

"That's enough. It's clear that you're jealous of Ace, and you should be. He's a better man than you'll ever be."

This Thug Love Got Me Trippin: A Belize Christmas

"That's sad because you really believe that nonsense," Knox laughed. "The ring on my pinky finger costs more than Ace's whole wardrobe. And that's the type of guy you want to be with? Someone who can't take care of you. A dude that you have to pick up and drive around. He must have some platinum dick because he don't have shit else going for him."

"His dick is better than yours," I admitted. "The last two times we fucked, I faked my orgasms. It wasn't good and I just didn't want to hurt your feelings."

"That's a lie."

"Sweetie, I don't have a reason to lie anymore. I'm not with you. Now, carry your ass on with Riley's lipstick on your collar and her scent all over you. Clearly, she's jealous of me because she had to stake her claim. If she only knew, I don't want your ass anymore."

I was done talking to Knox, so I started walking away. He grabbed me and I just blacked out, slapping the dog shit out of him. I didn't know if he was trying to attack me because of what I just said, so I reacted accordingly. Knox squealed loud as hell like a girl and then grabbed his face, backing away from me. I giggled all the way back inside. The high-pitched scream that Knox let out tickled me pink.

"What's so funny?" Ace asked.

I leaned into him and whispered, "I'll tell you later. You're going to crack up when I do."

Knox walked in a few seconds later and I cracked up.

"Can I have everyone's attention please?" Knox said with a huge red handprint across his cheek. "I have a confession."

It was as if everyone had stopped what they were doing and gave this asshole their undivided attention.

"What is he about to say this time?" Ace whispered.

"It would be nice if he said he was leaving early."

We chuckled a little too loudly and it caught Knox's attention. "Thank you everyone for your attention. I want to announce that Riley is pregnant."

I gasped and nearly choked. Not that I wanted him back because I didn't. I just realized that he was even more of a creep than what I thought.

"And my next announcement is about Ace."

"What about me?" Ace asked, piping up. "You don't know me, bro. I suggest you stay in your lane."

"You're right. I don't, bro, but apparently the department of corrections does."

It felt like I was about to have a heart attack when Knox pulled out a piece of paper and passed it around. When the folded up piece of paper got to me, I almost fainted. It was Ace's arrest record. I wasn't sure how Knox obtained all this information about Ace, but it had his whole life on one piece of paper. Listed for everyone to see it had all of his short comings.

"Is this true?" Eli asked Ace with disappointment.

"Oh, no, Ace," my mother said with the most disappointing look on her face. "I had high hopes for you, young man."

"Honey, I can't believe you've been lying to us," my father voice to me with a scowl. He glanced at Ace and squinted his eyes with contempt. "I think you need to leave."

"I'm, um, I'm sorry everyone. I never meant to hurt anyone. I just wanted Sassy to have a wonderful Christmas." Ace looked around the room with hurt. "I... I... you know what... never mind..." He walked out of the room before he could finish his sentence.

"I have a confession too," I stated after the shock wore off. "Knox has been hitting on me. He wanted me back yesterday and he just pulled me aside a few minutes ago to ask if I could be his side chick. When I wouldn't pick Ace over him, he decided to pull this scheme to expose Ace."

"Daughter," my father said. "Regardless of the fact, Ace is a criminal."

"Daddy, he's not a criminal. He's a good man who fell on hard times." I closed my eyes and blurted out. "I paid him to come here and be my fake boyfriend."

You could hear a pin drop. The whole room was so still, I was afraid to open my eyes. When I did, I saw the whole room watching me.

"That's right. I'll admit, I was so afraid to come here and face Christmas alone that I paid

This Thug Love Got Me Trippin: A Belize Christmas

Ace to be my boyfriend. The truth is, he's one of my clients."

"Clients!" my mother shrieked.

Knox and Riley laughed.

"What are you laughing at, bitch? You cheated with my fiancée when we were engaged. Just remember, how you got him is how you'll lose him. Knox still wants me and he's settling for you. You're a rebound, honey boo boo. And as for you Knox, I might have paid a man to spend the holidays with me, but I'm not a low down, filthy ass cheater who still wants his ex back. I moved on gracefully."

Riley looked as if she was about to lunge at me and I stood my ground. "You better get her, Knox. This ain't what she wants. I will beat her ass senseless."

"I think it's time for us to leave," Knox's father said.

Knox and his family said goodbye and I was more than ready for them to leave. Eli quickly moved on from the Ace fiasco. He looked more concerned with the naughty things Verde was whispering to him. I could tell it was naughty by their facial expressions and nasty body language.

Besides, Eli wasn't one to hold a grudge. He was too carefree for that. I wouldn't be surprised if Eli asked Ace to join him on the basketball court once he returned home.

My parents, on the other hand, were a different story. They were going to get to the bottom of everything. That's why I tried to sneak out and they caught me, summoning me to their villa to talk.

"Spill the beans, young lady," my mother scolded.

"Mom, you're always on me about having a man and getting pregnant before my eggs rot. I just didn't want to disappoint you."

"Don't give me that bull, young lady. You know that you could have come here alone and you would have been welcomed with open arms."

"Clara, I have told you not to hound that girl," my daddy defended. "Now, she done went and rented a nicca for Christmas." He shook his head. "A damn shame."

"I might have paid Ace to come, but I'm glad he did," I spat. "He's a really nice guy. I judged him at first the same way everyone else did, but he's treated me better in these last couple of days than Knox has our whole relationship. He even came into the bathroom while I was doing number two." I raised two fingers, showing my parents what I meant. "He was concerned. He was genuine. I might have paid him, but what he showed me money couldn't buy."

My mother smiled. "I won't deny that I really liked Ace. I didn't see him as being fake at all."

"He's not. What about you, daddy?"

"I don't know."

"Listen, Ace did me a favor and, whether things work out between us or not, I owe him. He made my Christmas fun and I will never forget that. I don't want Ace go to go to jail for a DUI. He made a mistake. He fell on hard times and I think he deserves a second chance."

My mother was already tearing up. "You remember when you got a DUI, Liam?" my mother announced.

I grabbed my chest dramatically and looked over at my daddy. "Really? Daddy, is this true?" I asked with a smirk. "You were a bad boy?"

My father just shook his head. "That was in the past."

"True, but mommy gave you a chance. I'm assuming this was before you came into money."

My mother tsked. "Chile, way before. Your father used to sell drugs and all that. He put us both through school with his dirty money. We wanted a better life and we did what we had to do."

"Ooooh," I remarked, staring at my daddy. "Is this true?"

My father reluctantly said, "I won't lie to you, baby girl. It's true."

"So, if I believe in Ace, why can't you give him a chance? Help him out and see if he can change the way you did."

"Let me and your mother think about it and we'll get back to you."

I kissed both of my parents. "I know that's a yes."

"I didn't say it was a yes," my father commanded.

"True, but I know it's a yes because I know you, dad. You say no easily."

"I'll see you all back home. My flight is earlier than yours."

This Thug Love Got Me Trippin: A Belize Christmas

I was on my way to see Ace and tell him the good news, but by the time I got to my villa, I sat my tired self down, and next thing I knew it was the next morning. I didn't even remember falling asleep.

"Shit!" I exclaimed when I noticed it was the next day.

I was sleeping so damn good too. Rapidly, I threw the covers off of me and rushed over to Ace's room. My heart dropped when I saw that he wasn't there and all his things were gone. On the bed was an envelope with my name on it and a note attached. I snatched them both up and read the note.

Dear Sassy,

Or should I call you Cassie lol. I thought you were the worst person when we met, but after spending Christmas with you and your family, I realize that you are a very special woman. I'm glad we met and got a chance to spend time together. I feel like we made a real connection, despite how things started off. I'm firing you as my fake girlfriend lol. I hope you find the man of your dreams. I left the money that I didn't spend in the envelope for you. I used some of it to change my flight back home and to get you all Christmas gifts. I plan on paying you back every dime as soon as I get a job. Take care.

P.S. Whatever you do you better not give Knox another chance or I'll kick your ass. *wink emoji* *crying laughing emoji*

Ace Boogie

I fumbled through the envelop of money and then fell across his bed, sobbing. It was at this moment that the pain that I felt was heartbreak. He was gone for real. I had been in denial for a hot minute about my feelings for Ace, but I knew without a doubt that I loved this man and I didn't want to lose him. I was going to do whatever it took to make things right between us. Even if we just remained as friends, I would be perfectly fine with that as long as we got to see each other.

Chapter 14

Ace Hood

I hadn't slept well since I left Belize. I thought about Sassy a million times since I left but, for once, I took my mother's advice. She always said that if you love someone, set them free, and if they come back to you, it was meant to be. That's what I did with Sassy. She needed to feel for me what I felt for her. As much as I didn't want to admit it, I felt the attraction since the courtroom. However, I didn't know anything about this love feeling, so I thought it was hatred.

It wasn't easy though. I knew she would be hurt when I packed my bags and took the boat back to the mainland. I wasn't afraid of her parents or their views of me. Nor was I afraid of what Knox had told them. Actually, I was about to tell her family the truth after dinner anyway. Knox just beat me to it. After I started to fall for Sassy, I realized that I had to come clean with her family. Whether she liked it or not. I wasn't a liar. Well, let me rephrase that. I didn't make it a habit of lying. That's what separated me from the next dude.

I heard all the things that Knox said the other night. That dude's heart was rotten. All he cared about was superficial things. Basically, he was hating on me because I was able to impress Sassy with just my personality. He probably flipped out like that because Sassy told him that she had a taste of this big dick. I couldn't blame him for pulling the only card he had. When dude's like that had their backs against the wall, they stooped low to prove a point. Knox brought up my issues because he was insecure with who he was and his love life. He thought that exposing my mistakes would win Sassy back. Even though I didn't stay to find out, I was positive that Sassy didn't fall for his washed up pimp ways. If you asked me, he wanted his cake and eat it too. Had I not shown up on this vacation, Sassy would have ended up being his main chick, with Riley being the side chick. They both would have been in a relationship with his player ass in two different houses.

"Ace! Are you up?" my mother yelled on the other side of my door.

"Yeah!"

"Well, your father and I don't want you to be late for court. Get yourself together so that this judge don't lock your ass up. We're coming with you to make sure."

"Okay," I announced.

My nerves were all over the place since I left Belize. I didn't tell my mother, but I hadn't been to sleep at all. I had been trying to block out my feelings for Sassy and our amazing experience in Belize. As soon as I got home, I did some serious soul searching. I thought about everything that had happened since the DUI until now. My life was fucked up. I needed to get it back in order. Everyone was calling, trying to hit me up, including Sassy, but I just needed a moment alone. I could be going to jail so alone time was exactly what I needed to reflect on my actions.

My heart was beating out of my chest.

Princess Diamond

Today was court day and a nicca was scared as a hooker in church. My fate was about to be determined. Was I going to jail without no bail until another court date was set? Or would the judge give me mercy and let me off with a slap on the wrist?

I drug myself out of bed with the worst attitude ever. I hadn't been able to reach my lawyer, leaving that nicca message after message. He never hit me back. He was probably still on vacation like most people do around this time of year. My case was one of thousands to him. I was just a number in his caseload and it showed. Then again, if he was going to show up to court and treat me the way Sassy did when we first met I was better off representing my damn self. I searched my phone, looking up previous DUI cases in Cook County, trying to prepare just in case I had to defend myself.

I sat in the courtroom while the judge ruled against other people's cases. My palms were sweaty and I made eye contact with the judge several times. She looked like she wasn't about to play with my ass. I didn't know if she woke up on the wrong side of the bed or what but, every time she banged her gavel, someone was being sentenced to jail.

Evidently, she had a fucked up Christmas because the woman that I met before the holiday seemed to have a heart. This angry ass woman before me was staring at folks like she was kin to Scrooge and the Grinch.

I kept looking around the courtroom, trying to see if I had legal counsel. Nope. Not a damn soul was there for me. Bowing my head, I said a silent prayer. My black ass was going to jail. I was sure of it. My mother noticed my nervousness. She scooted closer to me and began to pray.

"Father God, my son is a good kid. Yes, he's made some mistakes, but he deserves a chance to prove to the world that he is the son that we raised. As you know when one thing goes wrong, it can trigger a stream of bad choices and left turns. But, my God, the redeemer, the waymaker, the fixer, the one of grace and mercy, He who is above all can change anything around. I trust you Lord and my son knows you personally, so I'm sure that you have a plan for his life. No matter what the outcome is today, I just want your will to be done. Never leave Ace or forsake him and stay by his side through it all. We love you Lord. In Jesus' Name. Amen."

"Amen," I repeated. "Thanks, Ma. That's exactly what I needed. It feels like a weight has been lifted off my shoulders."

My name was called and I stood looking dapper. My father got me a new suit for Christmas and I decided to wear it for good luck. I needed all the prayer, luck, blessings, and any other well wishes people wanted to throw my way. Slowly, I walked up and took a seat in front of the judge.

"I hope you were able to obtain proper legal counsel since the last time I saw you?"

"Well, your honor, I um…" Nervously, I looked over at the officer who had arrested me. Damn, he was in court too, ready to testify and fry my ass.

"Where's your legal counsel, Mr. Hood?"

I sighed and put my head down when someone spoke up on my behalf.

"I'm right here your honor. I'm Ace Hood's legal representation. I'm sorry I'm late. I just obtained his services this morning."

This Thug Love Got Me Trippin: A Belize Christmas

The judge pulled her glasses down on her nose, looking over them. "You're excused this time. Don't let it happen again. I hope you're prepared."

"I am your honor."

All I can say is God still provides miracles. I ain't never seen this white man a day in my life, yet, he was in this courtroom representing me. I didn't see what direction he came from and he surely wasn't in the courtroom the last time I looked around. I heard my lawyer talking and I heard the judge speaking too. The police officer that arrested me, his voice was somewhere in the background too.

For real, at that moment, I was so overwhelmed. I didn't want to breakdown and sob right there in court, so I kind of blacked out, holding my head down. To some, my actions might have been disrespectful, but I did the only thing I could do… talk to God. I mumbled a little bit of prayer, a little bit of praise, and a little bit of thanks. I didn't stop my personal church service until I heard the judge call my name.

"Ace Hood, please rise."

My lawyer tapped me on the shoulder and I

stood up. On the outside, I looked cool but, on the inside, I was shaking like a leaf.

The judge took off her glasses and frowned. Then, there was a stare down. I wanted to look away, but I just wasn't built that way. I prayed. My mama prayed. Now, it was time for me to face the music like a man and deal with the consequences.

"I've heard from everyone but you. I want to hear your side of the story, young man," the judge stated.

I cleared my throat, trying to think of something slick to say. Nothing came to mind, so I decided to tell the truth.

"Judge, the last time I saw you, I was being defended by a woman who said that I was guilty. At that time, I took total offense to that statement because in my mind, I wasn't guilty. After reflecting on the situation, I come to the conclusion, she was right."

I heard several people gasp and comment behind me. It was so disturbing that the judge had to bang her gavel to quiet them down before I continued.

"Cassie Treyton was right. Just because I

didn't injure anyone or hurt myself or get into a wreck doesn't give me the right to get behind the wheel under the influence. What I did was stupid, selfless, and I wish I could take the whole incident back, but I can't so I'm willing to take whatever punishment you have for me."

"So, what I'm hearing you say is that you're remorseful?"

"Very much so," I said truthfully.

The judge stared at me again for a long time before she spoke again. "Case dismissed."

I stood there in shock. I heard her, but I really didn't expect her to dismiss my case.

"Go home and be with your family, Mr. Hood. And don't end up back in my courtroom or I'm going to send your butt to jail."

"Thank you so much, your honor," I stammered.

My lawyer turned to me and shook my hand firmly. I was just about to ask him who hired him and where did he come from because clearly, he wasn't a public defender. As I was about to open my mouth, I heard her voice.

"So, you mean to tell me, you almost got me disbarred and us both thrown in jail when you thought I was right all along?"

I turned around and there she was. Sassy was standing right in front of me. Honestly, I never thought I would see her again.

She hugged me tight. "I hired the lawyer for you with the money that you wouldn't take."

"Thanks, Sassy, I'm going to pay you back."

"I know you are and I have just the plan to help you get started. Eli told me all about your app. It's time to get that ball rolling."

When I stepped back from Sassy's embrace, I saw her parents talking to my parents and Eli walking towards us.

"What's up, bro?" he said, giving me a one arm hug.

"What's up, man?" I said with a wide grin. I hadn't smiled since I was in Belize.

"Oh and about that note you left. I'm glad you fired me as your fake girlfriend because I was hoping you could get to know me as your real girlfriend. What do you say?"

"I don't have anything to say, but I have something to show you."

This Thug Love Got Me Trippin: A Belize Christmas

I pulled her back into my arms and kissed her passionately, letting her know just how much I missed her.

Epilogue

One Year Later

anticipated app launch of the year. Not only were there pet owners there, pet lovers gathered to show their support as well. Walking onto the stage dressed in a tailor-made Italian suit, Ace Hood waved welcomingly at the crowd.

"Hello, everyone. My name is Ace Hood and I'm the creator of Fido, the dog app. It is a superior dog walking app that provides the largest 24/7 on-demand access to credited dog walkers based on breeds, needs, and schedules. You would be connected to a loving dog walker within thirty minutes maximum. Recurring services can be requested as well. For an additional fee, a GPS tracer feature will be issued and a puppy report. Also for an additional charge, dog sitters and boarding service are offered in your area. The users can pay a one-time fee for the services or a monthly subscription. It's available in Android and iPhone as well."

The crowd cheered as the screen behind him lit up with a picture of the app on the screen.

"Although we have officially been in business in London, today is the official launch day for the U.S. app and I couldn't be more excited. Without any further delay, let me introduce you to Fido."

Ace stepped to the side so that everyone could see the screen clearly. "How did I do?" he asked Sassy.

"You were amazing," she said, kissing him on the lips. "No one would ever know that you stayed up all last night trying to memorize what you wanted to say."

Ace turned up his lip. "Don't act like you weren't nervous too."

"I was just a little bit, but I knew you were going to knock it out the park."

"True. You know there is nothing I can't do."

"Whatever. Here you go with that nonsense again."

"You know it's true. I'll prove it to you. Do you think we have enough time to get in a quickie before the video goes off?"

"No, we don't, nasty"

"Don't act like you don't want this thug loving," Ace smirked.

Sassy always wanted his thug loving, but right now wasn't the right time to get it. "Boy, go ahead. The video is going off now."

Sassy playfully slapped his arm. "Get your butt back out there."

Ace winked at Sassy and cheerfully walked back on stage with a pep in his step. The app was already a million-dollar business from the success that he had in London. Now, that it was in the U.S., it was projected that profits would go up 200%

"So, what do you think?" Ace coolly asked the crowd.

Cheers and rumbles of approval could be heard from all over the room.

"We have more in store to show you and actual testers of the app that you can play around with on the other side of the exhibit hall but,

This Thug Love Got Me Trippin: A Belize Christmas

before we get in to the rest of the program, I have to publicly thank someone special."

Ace looked backstage and waved Sassy to come forward. Shyly, she walked up on stage and stood next to him. He slipped his hand into hers and stared at her with loving eyes.

"This is Cassie Treyton. She's a lawyer by the way for Saxon & Baker, just in case y'all wanted to know. I got a smart woman who wins court cases," he joked.

Everyone shared a laugh with him.

"Isn't she beautiful y'all? Turn around baby and show off that dress."

Ace laughed and the crowd knew that he was joking around with the love of his life. Sassy blushed and mouthed thank you to everyone. She was going to kill Ace for putting her on the spot like this. Although her gown was gorgeous and she looked flawless, she felt uncomfortable speaking in public unless it pertained to law.

"No, but seriously, if it wasn't for this woman right here, I wouldn't be where I am today," Ace boasted, making Sassy blush.

Princess Diamond

"God answers prayers and dreams definitely come true. Believe it or not, when I met this intelligent woman, I was in jail."

Some of the audience was shocked. Others had heard the story before, so they weren't surprised.

"And believe it or not, we hated each other."

Ace snickered and Sassy slapped his arm, taking the microphone away from him to say a quick word.

"Don't let Ace charm you. He was hating on me because I was right and he was wrong."

She giggled and everyone burst into laughter with her.

Ace shrugged. "I won't even dare to defend myself. She argues with people for a living. I won't win."

More laughter.

"Long story short, she hired me to be her fake boyfriend to get her old boyfriend back and during that Christmas vacation to Belize, we fell in love."

All that could be heard was ooooohs and aaaaahs.

This Thug Love Got Me Trippin: A Belize Christmas

"The bible says he who finds a wife finds a good thing. Well, I believe that saying with all of my heart."

Ace let go of Sassy's hand and got down on one knee. He opened the Tiffany jewelry box and revealed the ring that she pointed out several months ago when they were window shopping.

"A year ago, I was broke with nothing and I couldn't even afford to glance at a ring like this. Still, you stood by my side during the worst time of my life and you supported me, defended me, believed in me, and loved me. I couldn't think of anyone else that deserves this ring and who I would want to be my wife. Cassie Sassy Treyton, will you marry me?"

Tears had already started to fall as Sassy stared at Ace. She was truly caught off guard. Things were going so well with them. They were friends as well as lovers and, as bad as she wanted to be engaged in the past, the thought never crossed her mind while she was with Ace. Things between them just felt so right. After his DUI case was thrown out, they concentrated on having fun and leveling up. Her mission was to get employed at Saxon & Baker while Ace worked extra hard at finding a temporary job until Fido took off. Although he didn't take what Knox said to heart, he wanted to be a great provider for Sassy and make his parents and her parents proud.

"Yes, of course, I'll marry you. I wouldn't want to spend my life with anyone else but you."

Everyone cheered as Ace stood up and kissed Sassy on the lips.

"I love you, Sassy."

"I love you, Ace Boogie."

The End

Happy Holidays

CPSIA information can be obtained
at www.ICGtesting.com
Printed in the USA
LVHW111525181219
640938LV00003B/436/P